The Priceless Pearl

Alice Duer Miller

Alpha Editions

This edition published in 2024

ISBN 9789362097552

Design and Setting By

Alpha Editions
www.alphaedis.com

Email - info@alphaedis.com

As per information held with us this book is in Public Domain.
This book is a reproduction of an important historical work.
Alpha Editions uses the best technology to reproduce historical work
in the same manner it was first published to preserve its original nature.
Any marks or number seen are left intentionally to preserve.

Contents

CHAPTER I .... - 1 -

CHAPTER TWO .... - 25 -

CHAPTER THREE .... - 44 -

CHAPTER FOUR .... - 66 -

CHAPTER I

"The girl is simply too good-looking," said Bunner, the office manager, in a high, complaining voice. "She is industrious, intelligent, punctual and well-mannered, but simply too good-looking—a disturbing element in the office on account of her appearance. I made a grave mistake in engaging her."

The president, who had been a professor of botany at a great university before he resigned in order to become head of The Universal Encyclopedia of Necessary Knowledge Publishing Corporation, was a trifle deaf, but had not as yet admitted the fact to himself; and he inquired with the patient, slightly contemptuous surprise of the deaf, "But I do not understand why she is crying."

"It is not she who is crying," answered the office manager regretfully; "it is Mr. Rixon, our third vice president. He is crying because he has most unfortunately become interested in the young woman—fallen in love with her—so my stenographer tells me."

The president peered through his bifocal lenses. He did not wish to be thought one of those unsophisticated scientists who understand only the plain unpsychological process of plants. He inquired whether the girl had encouraged the third vice president, whether, in a word, she had given him to understand that she took a deeper interest in him than was actually the fact, "the disappointment of the discovery being the direct cause of the emotional outbreak which you have just described."

Bunner hesitated. He would have liked to consider that Miss Leavitt was to blame, for otherwise the responsibility was entirely his own. In his heart he believed she was, for he was one of those men who despise women and yet consider them omnipotent.

"I can't say I've ever seen her do more than say good morning to him," he answered rather crossly. "But I believe there is a way of avoiding a man—with her appearance. You have probably never noticed her, sir, but——"

"Oh, I've noticed her," said the president, nodding his old head. "I've noticed a certain youth and exuberant vitality, and—yes, I may say beauty—decided beauty."

Bunner sighed.

"A girl like that ought to get married," he said. "They ought not to be working in offices, making trouble. It's hard on young men of susceptible natures like Mr. Rixon. You can hardly blame him."

No, they agreed they did not blame him at all; and so they decided to let the young woman have her salary to the first of the month and let her go immediately.

"That will be best, Bunner," said the president, and dismissed the matter from his mind.

But Bunner, who knew that there was a possibility that even a beautiful young woman might not enjoy losing her job, could not dismiss the matter from his mind until the interview with her was over. He decided, therefore, to hold it at once, and withdrew from the president's room, where, as a directors' meeting was about to take place, the members of the board were already beginning to gather.

Bunner was a pale fat man of forty, who was as cold to the excessive emotion of the third vice president as he was to the inconvenient beauty which had caused it. He paused beside Miss Leavitt's desk in the outer office and requested a moment of her time.

She had finished going over the article on Corals and was about to begin that on Coronach—a Scotch dirge or lamentation for the dead. She had just been wondering whether any created being would ever want to know anything about coronach, when Mr. Bunner spoke to her. If she had followed her first impulse she would have looked up and beamed at him, for she was of the most friendly and warmhearted nature; but she remembered that beaming was not safe where men were concerned—even when they were fat and forty—so she answered coldly, "Yes, Mr. Bunner," and rose and followed him to his own little office.

Miss Pearl Leavitt, A. B., Rutland College, was not one of those beauties who must be pointed out to you before you appreciate their quality. On the contrary, the eye roving in her neighborhood was attracted to her as to a luminary. There was nothing finicky or subtle or fine-drawn about her. Her features were rather large and simple, like a Greek statue's, though entirely without a statue's immobility. Her coloring was vivid—a warm brunette complexion, a bright golden head and a pair of large gray eyes that trembled with their own light as they fixed themselves upon you, much as the reflection of the evening star trembles in a quiet pool. But what had always made her charm, more than her beauty, was her obvious human desire to be a member of the gang—to enjoy what the crowd enjoyed and do what was being done. It was agony to her to assume the icy, impassive demeanor which, since she had been working in offices, she had found necessary. But she did it. She was hard up.

When Mr. Bunner had sent away his stenographer and shut the door he sat down and pressed his small fat hands together.

"Miss Leavitt," he said, "I am sorry to be obliged to tell you that during the summer months when so many of our heads of departments are away on their vacations, we shall be obliged to reduce our office staff; and so, though your work has been most satisfactory—we have no complaint to make of your work—still I am sorry to be obliged to tell you that during the summer months, when so many of our heads of departments——"

He did not know what was the matter; the sentence appeared to be a circular sentence without exits.

Miss Leavitt folded her arms with a rapid whirling motion. Of course, since the first three words of his sentence she had known that she had lost her job.

"Just why is it that I am being sent away?" she said.

Sulky children, before they actually burst into tears, have a way of almost visibly swelling like a storm cloud. It would be wrong to suggest that anything as lovely as Pearl Leavitt could swell, and yet there was something of this effect as she stared down at the office manager. He did not like her tone, nor yet her look.

He said with a sort of acid smile, "I was about to explain the reason when you interrupted me. Although your work has been perfectly satisfactory, we feel that during the summer months——" He wrenched himself away from that sentence entirely. "It is the wish of the president," he said, "that you be given your salary to the first of the month—which I hereby hand you—and be told that it will not be necessary for you to come here after today. In parting with you, Miss Leavitt, I wish to assure you that the quality of your work for this organization has been in every respect——"

"I want to speak to the president," said Miss Leavitt.

She did not raise her voice, but no one could have mistaken that her tone was threatening. She vibrated her head slightly from side to side, and spit out her $t's$ in a way actually alarming to Bunner, who was a man susceptible to fear.

"Our decision is quite final—quite final, I'm sorry to say," he said, fussing with his papers as a hint that she had better go and leave him in peace.

"That's why I want to speak to him."

"Quite impossible," answered Bunner. "The board is meeting at present in his room——"

"What!" cried Pearl. "They're all there together, are they?" And before the office manager took in her intention she was out of his office, across the main office and in the board room.

Like so many people destined to succeed in New York, Pearl came originally from Ohio. She was an orphan, and after her graduation from an Eastern college she had gone back to her native state, meaning to make her home with her two aunts. It had not been a successful summer. Not only was it hot, and there was no swimming where her aunts lived, and Pearl loved to swim, but two of her cousins fell in love with her—one from each family—and it became a question either of their leaving home or of her going. So Pearl very gladly came East again, and under the guidance of her great friend Augusta Exeter began to look for a job.

She had come East in September, and it was now July—hardly ten months—and yet in that time she had had and lost four good jobs through no fault of her own but wholly on account of her extraordinary beauty. She was not insulted; no one threatened her virtue or offered to run away with her. It was simply that, like Helen of Troy, "Where'er she came she brought calamity."

Her first place had been with a publishing firm, Dixon & Gregory. When Pearl came to them the business was managed by the two sons of the original firm; the elder Dixon was dead, and the elder Gregory, a man of fifty-six or eight, came to the office only once or twice a week. A desk for her had been put in his private room, as it was almost always vacant. It ceased, however, to be vacant as soon as he saw Pearl. He had no idea that he had fallen in love with her—perhaps he had not. He certainly never troubled, her with attentions; as far as she knew he was hardly aware of her existence. His emotion, whatever it was, took the form of quarreling with anyone who did speak to her—even in the course of necessary business. When at last one day he met her and the younger Dixon going out to lunch at the same hour and in the same elevator, but purely by accident, he made such a violent and inexplicable scene that the two younger partners, after consultation, decided that the only thing to do was to get rid of the girl quietly—get her to resign. They were both very nice about it, and themselves found her another place—as secretary to a magazine editor—a man of ice, they assured her. She never saw the elder Mr. Gregory again, and a few months later read in the papers of his death.

Her new position went well for several months. The editor was, as represented, a man of ice; but, as Hamlet has observed, being as pure as snow and as chaste as ice does not protect against calumny, and the wife of the editor, entering the office one day to find her husband and his secretary bending over an illegible manuscript, refused to allow such dangerous beauty so near her husband, and Pearl lost her second job.

Her next place was with an ambitious young firm which was putting a new cleaning fluid on the market. At first, in a busy office, Pearl seemed to pass almost unnoticed. Then one day the two partners, young men both and heretofore like brothers, came to her together and asked her if she would do the firm a great favor—sit for her portrait to a well-known artist so that they might use her picture as a poster to advertise their product. Pearl consented—she thought it would be rather good fun. The result was successful. Indeed, the only criticism of the picture—which represented Pearl in tawny yellow holding up a saffron-colored robe at which she smiled brilliantly, with beneath it the caption, Why Does She Smile? Because Her Old Dress is Made New by—was that it would have been better to get a real person to sit for the picture, as the public was tired of these idealized types of female beauty. But the trouble started over who was to own the original pastel. It developed that each partner had started the idea from a hidden wish to own a portrait of Pearl. They quarreled bitterly. The very existence of the firm was threatened. An old friend of the two families stepped in and effected a reconciliation, but his decision was that the girl must go. It did not look well for two boys of their age—just beginning in business—to have as handsome a woman as that in the office. People might talk.

It was after this—some time after—that Pearl took the place with the Encyclopedia company. Her record began to tell against her. Everyone wanted to know why she changed jobs so often. She thought she had learned her lesson—not to beam, not to be friendly, not to do anyone favors. She had made up her mind to stay with the Encyclopedia forever. She had had no hint of danger. She hardly knew the third vice president by sight—someone in the office had told her a silly story about his crying one day, but she hadn't even believed it. And now she had lost another job—and in July, too, when jobs are hard to find.

Heretofore she had always gone docilely. But now she felt she could bear it no longer—she must tell someone what she thought.

It was four o'clock on a hot summer afternoon, and round the board-room table the members were saying "aye" and "no" and "I so move," while their minds were occupied with the questions that do occupy the mind at such times—golf and suburban trains, and whether huckleberry pie in hot weather hadn't been a mistake—when the glass door opened and a beautiful girl came in like a hurricane. She had evidently been talking for some seconds when she entered. She was saying, "——are just terrible. I want to tell you gentlemen, now that I have you together, that I think men are just terrible." She had a curious voice, deep and a little rough, more like a boy's than a woman's, yet a voice which when you once knew Pearl you remembered with affection. "This is the fourth job I've lost because men have no self-control. I do my work. I don't even speak to any of you—I'd like to—I'm human, but I don't dare any more. I attend to business, there's no fault found with my work—but I've got to go because some man or other can't work in the office with me. Why not? Because he has no self-control—and not ashamed of it—not ashamed, that's what shocks me. Why, if a girl found she couldn't do her work because there was a good-looking man in the office, she'd die rather than admit she was so silly. But what does a man do? He goes whining to the president to get the poor girl dismissed. There it is! I have to go!"

And so on, and so on. The board was so astonished at her entrance, at the untrammeled way in which she was striding up and down, digging her heels into the rug and flinging her arms about as she talked, that they were like people stunned. They turned their eyes with relief to Mr. Bunner, who came hurrying in behind her.

"Miss Leavitt has been dropped," he began, but she cut him short.

"I've been dropped," she said, "because———"

"Will you let me speak?" said Mr. Bunner—a rhetorical question. He meant to speak in any case.

"No," answered Pearl. "Certainly not. Gentlemen, I have been dismissed—I know—because some man in this office has no self-control. I can't identify him, but I have my suspicions." And she cast a dreadful glance at the third vice president. "Why should I go? Why shouldn't he? Crying! Woof! How absurd!"

"Leave the room, Miss Leavitt," said the president; but he weakened the effect of his edict by leaning forward with his hand to his ear so as to catch whatever she was going to say next.

"I haven't shed a tear since my mother died," said Mr. Rixon rather tearfully to the man next him.

"This is not the time to discuss your grievance, Miss Leavitt," said the treasurer, wondering why he had never kept in closer touch with the office; "but if you feel you have a just complaint against the company come to my office tomorrow afternoon———"

"I'll not go near your office," said Pearl, and she began again to stride about the room, occasionally stamping her right foot without losing step. "I shall never again go into any office where men are. I won't work for men. They're poor sports; they have no self———"

"You said that before," said the treasurer.

"———control," Pearl went on, for people in her frame of mind cannot be stopped. "Why shouldn't he go? But no, you have to be protected from a girl like a herd of sheep from a wolf—a girl who hasn't even looked at you, at that. If I had ever spoken to the man——"

"Leave the room instantly, Miss Leavitt," said the president, and this time he spoke as if he meant it, for he was afraid the identity of the third vice president might be revealed. Little it mattered to Pearl what the old man meant.

"I wouldn't mind so much," she went on, "if you did not all pretend to be so brave and strong—to protect women. You protect each other—that's who you protect."

"Come, come," said a member of the board. "This isn't the way to keep a job, you know."

"I don't want to keep this job. I want you for once to hear what a woman thinks of the men she works for—a lot of poor sports—and not industrious—none of you work the way girls work for you. Slack, that's what I call you, and lacking in self-control."

And she went out as suddenly as she had come in, and slammed the door so hard behind that those members of the board, sitting near it ducked their heads into their collars in fear of falling glass.

There was a minute's pause, and then the president said with a slight smile, "Well, Mr. Bunner, I think we all see what you meant when you said this young woman was a disturbing element in the office."

"There has never been anything like this before," said Bunner; "never anything in the least like this anywhere I have ever been."

"Well," said the treasurer, "I don't suppose we need distress ourselves about her finding another job."

There was a certain wistful undercurrent in his tone.

"No," said Bunner, slightly misunderstanding his meaning. "She is competent and industrious."

"She ought to get married, a pretty girl like that—not go about making trouble in offices," said the president.

"I have always been of the opinion," said the third vice president, "that it would be much simpler to run the office entirely with men."

"Oh, it would be much better—much better, of course," said Bunner; "only women are so much more accurate about detail, more industrious and less expensive."

And as there was no woman present to inquire why then men were so much more desirable, the question dropped, and the president recalled the board's attention to the subject of the paper to be used in their next edition—the topic under consideration when Pearl made her entrance. It was rather hard to take any interest in it now.

And so Pearl began once again to go the round of agencies, to interview or be interviewed by office managers, and hear that if she came back in October there might be a chance. But October was three months away, and she could not live three months on something less than a hundred dollars. She even began to scan the columns of the newspapers—from clerks, through stenographers, ushers, and finally winders—she never found out what winders were.

If her dear friend and sage adviser, Augusta Exeter, had been in town she could have shared her room; but Augusta was in Vermont, visiting the family of the man she was going to marry. At least, Augusta's last letter had been from Vermont; but as a matter of fact, three days after Pearl left the Encyclopedia's employ Augusta came back to New York. She had had a letter from the agency where her name was registered practically offering a position which sounded too good to refuse. Besides, Augusta did not really like farm life in Vermont, and the Baynes family, for some reason which she could not explain, gave her a composite picture of Horace, her fiancé, which tended to make her love him less. Even New York in midsummer was preferable.

Therefore it happened that as Pearl wandered, lonely as a cloud, from office to office, longing for her friend's wisdom, Augusta herself was sitting in the outer office of a company, looking for a job.

Though the office was that of the Finlay-Wood Engineering Co., the position which Miss Augusta Exeter was considering was that of a governess. She was not at all sure that she wanted the place. College women are not well disposed toward positions as governesses; yet as Miss Exeter sat there in the busy outer office and watched the office boys coming in and out, and the impassive young woman at the switchboard, enunciating again and again, "Finlay-Wood Company," "Hold the wire," she went over the advantages of this offer—a high salary, the two hottest months of the summer at Southampton, and the fact that as she was to be married in October, she could not take a long-time position in any case.

Mr. Wood's secretary, with whom so far all the negotiations had been carried on, had impressed upon her the necessity of being punctual— "eleven precisely," he had said, for it seemed Mr. Wood was going to Mexico that afternoon. And so Augusta, who was punctual by nature, had found herself in the office ten minutes ahead of time. She sat listening to the telephone girl and watching a door which bore the simple inscription, "Mr. Wood." And just behind that door a tall sunburned man in the neighborhood of thirty was standing, slapping the pockets of his blue serge clothes and saying, "Griggs, I have a feeling I've forgotten something. What is it I've forgotten, Griggs?"

The desk was as bare as a desk ought to be when its owner is going away for two months. Griggs ran his eye proudly over it.

"No, Mr. Wood," he said. "I don't think anything has been forgotten. Nothing was left except the letter to the President, the Spanish dictionary and the Mexican currency. All that has been attended to."

He consulted a list held in the palm of his hand.

"It was something of my own," said Wood, and he eyed his secretary with an air that might have appeared stern but was merely concentrated, when the door opened and the office boy came in and said, "Miss Stone says she's notified him that there's a lady there to see him, and will we let her in to him?"

"A lady?" said Griggs severely.

"That's it," said Wood. "It's the governess for my sister. Think of my nearly forgetting that!"

"You ought not be worried about such things," said Griggs, as if he were very bitter about it, "with all your responsibilities."

Wood smiled. It wasn't true, but it was the way one's secretary ought to feel.

"I'd have a lot more to worry me," he said, "if I were married myself."

"You certainly would," answered Griggs, who was married.

"But will we let her in to him?" said the office boy, who clung to this formula, although the head clerk was trying to break him of it.

"You may let her come in," said Griggs, as if he would perish rather than allow his chief to hold verbal communication with anything so low as an office boy, and as he spoke he silently gave Wood a pale-blue card—one of a dozen on which in beautiful block letters he had written down the names, degrees, past experience, with notes on personal appearance, of all the candidates for position of governess in the household of Wood's sister, Mrs. Conway.

"This is the best of them?" said Wood, and he ran his eye rapidly over the card, which read:

"Augusta Exeter, A. B. Rutland College; Ph. D., Columbia University, specialized in mathematics and household management."

He looked up. "Queer combination, isn't it?"

"I thought it was just what you wanted," answered Griggs reproachfully.

"Nothing queerer than that," said Wood, and went on: "Six-month dietary expert—one year training—appearance, pleasing." He glanced at his secretary. It amused him to think of the discreet Griggs appraising the appearance of these young women. "What system did you mark them on, Griggs?" he asked, but got no further, for the door opened and Miss Exeter entered, and Griggs, with his unfailing discretion, left.

Wood looked at her and saw that Griggs as usual had been exactly right—she was neither more nor less than pleasing—a small, slim, pale girl, whose unremarkable brown eyes radiated a steady intelligence.

Wood had employed labor in many parts of the world, from Chile to China, and he had a routine about it—a preliminary intelligence test, which he applied.

"Sit down, Miss Exeter," he said. "I think it will save us both time if you will tell me all that you know about this position"—this was the test—"and then I'll fill in."

Augusta sat down. She found herself a trifle nervous. This man impressed her, for since her childhood she had cherished a secret romantic admiration for men who exercised any form of power—kings and generals and men of great affairs. It was a feeling that had nothing to do with real life and represented no disloyalty to her fiancé, Horace Bayne, who exercised no power of any kind.

One reason why it had had no relation to life was that she had not met any men of this type. Even in the outer office she had been impressed by the sense of a man waited on and protected by secretaries and office boys as an Eastern princess is waited upon by slaves. And now when she saw him she saw that he had exactly the type of looks she admired most—tall, a little too thin, his face tanned to that shade of *café au lait* that the blond Anglo-Saxon acquires under the sun—those piercing bright-blue eyes—that large handsome hand, which, with the thumb in his waistcoat pocket, was so clearly outlined against the blue serge of his clothes.

She said rather uncertainly, "I know that Mrs. Conway is a widow with three children——"

Even this much was wrong.

"Not, a widow," he said; "divorced."

"——with three children," Augusta went on; "a girl of seventeen, a boy of fifteen and a little girl of eleven. I know that during your absence you want someone to take the care and responsibility of the children off your sister's shoulders."

He smiled—his teeth seemed to have the extraordinary whiteness that is the compensation of a dark skin.

"I see," he said, "that Griggs has been discreet again." He glanced at his watch. "I'm going to Mexico in a few hours, Miss Exeter. I have just twenty-five minutes. If in that time I am not thoroughly indiscreet I can't look to you for any help. The situation is this: My sister married Gordon Conway when she was very young—eighteen; he turned out to be a gambler. I don't know whether you've ever known any gamblers"—Miss Exeter never had—"but they are a peculiar breed—the real ones—charming—friendly—gay—open-handed when they are winning; they become the most inhuman devils in the world when they are losing. Never get tied up to a gambler. During my poor sister's romance and marriage Conway was winning—large sums—on the races. But that stopped a month or so after their marriage, and ever since then, as far as I know, he has lost—in stocks, at Monte Carlo, and finally at every little gambling casino in Europe. After about six years of it we managed to get her a divorce. She has entire control of the children, of course. Conway has sunk out of sight. Oh, once in a while he turns up and tries to get a little money from her, but fortunately what little she inherited from my father came to her after her divorce, or otherwise he'd have managed to get it away from her. She's very generous—weak—whichever you call it. One of the things I'm going to ask you to do is to prevent her seeing him at all, and certainly prevent her letting him have any money. Though it isn't likely to happen. I believe he's abroad.

"The great point is the children. I'm sorry to say that it seems to me my sister is ruining three naturally fine children as rapidly as a devoted mother can. Of course, many parents are over indulgent, but my sister not only indulges her children but gives them at the same time the conviction that they are such interesting and special types that none of the ordinary rules apply to them. The elder girl, Dorothy, is a pretty, commonplace American girl—no fault to find with her except that her mother treats her as if she were an empress. If, for instance, her mother keeps her waiting five minutes she behaves as if she were an exiled queen faced by treachery among her dependents—won't speak to her mother perhaps for a day. And if I say—which I oughtn't to do, for it's no use—'Isn't Dorothy a trifle insolent?' my sister answers, 'I'm so delighted to see that she isn't growing up with the inferiority complex that I had as a girl.' The boy is a perfectly straight manly boy, but he smokes constantly—at fifteen—and when I criticize him my sister says before him, 'Well, Anthony, you know you smoke yourself. I can't very well tell Durland it's a crime. Besides, I have the theory that if he smokes enough now he'll be tired of it by the time he grows up.'"

"But that isn't sound," said Miss Exeter, quite shocked at the sketch she was hearing. "Habits formed in youth———"

"Of course it isn't sound," said Wood. "And as a matter of fact, my sister never thought of it until I objected. She evolves these theories merely for the sake of protecting her children. Oddly enough, she not only doesn't want to change them herself but she doesn't want any one else to change them. Three years ago I engaged in a life-and-death struggle with her to get Durland—the boy—to boarding school. She advanced the following arguments against it: First, that he was a perfectly normal, manly boy and did not need to go; second, that he was of a peculiar, artistic, sensitive temperament and would be wrecked by being made to conform to boarding-school standards; third, that none of the successful men of the country had gone to boarding school; fourth, that success was the last thing she desired for any son of hers; fifth, that she did not wish to remove him from the benefits of my daily influence; and sixth, that I was a person of no judgment and absolutely wrong about its being wise for a boy to go to school."

"And is he at school?" Miss Exeter inquired politely.

"Oh, yes," answered Wood, without seeing anything amusing in her question. "Although my sister does a good deal to counteract the effect—by making fun of the teachers and the rules, and always bringing him, when she goes to visit him, whatever is specially forbidden, like candy and cigarettes and extra pocket money. You see, that's where it's going to be hard for you. She not only doesn't want to discipline them herself but she's against any person or institution that tries to do it for her. As soon as you begin to accomplish anything with the children—as I'm sure you will do—she'll be against you; she'll want you to go."

"That makes it pretty hopeless, doesn't it?" said Miss Exeter.

He shook his head briskly.

"No," he said; "for I have made her promise that she won't send you away, no matter what happens, until I get back. I know what was in her mind when she gave the promise—that she could make it so unpleasant for you that you'd go of your own accord. So, Miss Exeter, I want you to promise me that you won't go, no matter how disagreeable she makes it———"

"Oh, Mr. Wood, I couldn't do that," said Augusta.

"There's no use in going at all otherwise," he said. "Oh, come, be a sport! I'll make it worth while. I'll give you a bonus of five hundred dollars if you're still on the job when I get back—or I'll bring you a turquoise—I'm going down to inspect the best mine in the world. You see, I feel this means the whole future of those children—to be with a woman like you. I know you could do with them just what I want done."

"You may be mistaken about that, Mr. Wood."

"I may be, but I'm not."

The blue eyes fixed themselves on her. She said to herself that it was the five hundred dollars—so desirable for a trousseau—that turned the scale, but the blue eyes and the compliment had something to do with her decision.

"It seems a reckless thing to promise," she murmured with a weak laugh.

"No, not at all. I wouldn't let you do anything reckless." He spoke as a kindly grandfather might speak. "And now we have ten minutes left, and I want to talk to you about the little one—Antonia." His face softened, and after a slight struggle he yielded to a smile. "The truth is," he said, "that she's much my favorite. She's intelligent and honest, and the justest person of any age or sex that I ever knew in my life." He paused a second. "Perhaps it is because I'm fonder of her than of the other two, but it seems to me my sister is particularly unwise about Antonia."

His mind went back to his parting the evening before with this small niece. He and his sister had been sitting on the piazza of the house they had taken at Southampton—at least she had taken it and he had paid for it. Only a few yards away the Atlantic, in one of its placid lakelike moods, was hissing slowly up and down on the sand. The struggle about a governess had been going on for several weeks. So far Mrs. Conway had won, for this was his last evening and none had been engaged. She had a wonderful method for dealing with her brother—a method to be commended to all weak people trying to get the maximum of interest and the minimum of control from stronger natures. She listened to everything he said as if she were wholly convinced by his words and intended to follow his advice to the last detail, and then she went away and did just what she had always meant to do. If he reproached her she looked at him wonderingly and said: "But, Anthony dear, I did agree with you at the time; but afterward, when I came to think——" Oh, how well he knew that dread phrase, "afterward, when I came to think!"

By these methods she had managed to fend off action for three weeks, agreeing with him most cordially that the children ought to have a governess, but thinking, after he had gone to New York for the week, that it would be nice for them to take French lessons with that charming French lady in the village, or that perhaps the Abernathys' governess would come over for an hour a day——

And now on his last evening he had outmaneuvered her by announcing that he was interviewing candidates the next morning before he took his train, and would send her the best.

"I'm sure it's very kind of you to take all this trouble, Tony," she said. "Don't send me anyone too hideous, will you?"

"Griggs describes the young woman I have in mind as of pleasing appearance."

"That means perfectly hideous."

"You wouldn't want a prize beauty, would you?"

"Certainly I would. I like to have lovely things about me. I suppose you think that's idiotic."

He assured her that he never thought her idiotic—at least not unintentionally—and went on to obtain the famous pledge—the promise that she would keep the governess he sent her until his return in September. She agreed finally, partly because it was getting late and she was sleepy, partly because she reflected that there were more ways of getting rid of governesses than by sending them away.

"I'm so sleepy," she said, yawning, "and yet I don't quite like to go to bed until Antonia comes in."

"Antonia?" said Wood. "I thought she went to bed at nine."

It appeared that Antonia had formed the habit lately of sleeping on the beach—at least for the earlier part of the night—just digging a hole and curling up there. Her mother thought it an interesting, primitive, healthy sort of instinct.

"And yet," she added thoughtfully, as if she knew she were a little finicky, "I don't like to lock up the house until she comes in."

"I think you're right," said her brother. These were the things that terrified him so—a little girl out in the blackness of that beach in her pajamas. How could he go to Mexico and leave her? He rose and went to the edge of the piazza, which rested on the dunes.

He could see nothing but the stars.

"Shall I call her?" he said.

"I hate to wake her; but—yes, just give a call."

He shouted, and in a few seconds a faint, cheerful hullo reached them, and a little figure appeared over the dunes.

"Were you asleep, darling?" said her mother.

"No, I was swimming," said Antonia. She stepped within the circle of light from the windows, and Wood could see that her dark curly hair was plastered to her head, and her pajamas clung to her like tissue paper. "I love to swim at night," she said. "It makes you feel like a spirit."

She shared her more important thoughts with her uncle. Then, turning to her mother, she advanced toward her with outstretched arms as if to clasp her in a wet embrace.

"Look out for your mother's dress," said Wood, for Edna Conway was as usual perfectly dressed in white. She smiled at him and took the child to her breast.

"Dear Anthony," she said, "if you were married you'd know that a woman loves her children better than her clothes."

He was silent, wondering if she knew how much she had had to do with the fact that he wasn't married. He had no taste for masculine women, and yet Edna had made him distrustful of all femininity which sooner or later developed the sweet obstinacy, the clinging pig-headedness, the subtle ability, under the idiotic coyness of a kitten, to get its own way. Well off and physically attractive, he had not been neglected by women, but always sooner or later it had seemed to him that he had seen the dread shadow of kittenishness. Cattishness he could have borne, but the kitten in woman disgusted him.

"And, dearest," his sister was saying to her daughter, "you won't go to bed in your wet things, will you?"

Antonia shook her finger at her mother.

"Now don't begin to be fussy," she said, not impudently, but as one equal gives advice to another. Yet even this mild suggestion of reproof was painful to Edna.

She turned to her brother and said passionately, "I'm not fussy, am I? I don't see how you can say that, Antonia. It's only that your uncle wouldn't close an eye if he thought you were sleeping in damp pajamas; would you, Anthony?" And she laughed gayly.

This was one of her most irritating ways—to pretend that she was just a wild thing like the children, but that to oblige some stuffy older person she was forced to ask the children to conform.

"I might close an eye, at that," said Anthony.

The whole incident had finally decided him to take the prospective governess entirely into his confidence. He had thought at first it would be more honorable to let her discover the situation for herself, but now he saw that she would need not only all his knowledge of the situation but the full conviction that he was backing her, whatever she did. He became convinced of this even before he saw Miss Exeter. Having seen her, he had no further hesitation. He thought her as sensible a person as he had ever met. She sat there in the hard north light of his office, noting down now and then a few words in a little black notebook. She was not only sensible—she was to be depended on.

"The truth is," he said, "that Antonia, not to put too fine a point on it, is not personally clean."

Miss Exeter smiled, for to her mind the tone of agony in his voice was exaggerated.

"But at a certain age no children are," she said.

"But most children are forced to be, and my sister lets this child run wild, so that people talk about it. I suppose I oughtn't to mind so much," he said, looking at her rather wistfully; "but you can't imagine how I hate to think that people discuss Antonia's being dirty. And all my sister says is that she's so glad the child isn't vain. Oh, Miss Exeter, if you could get Antonia dressed like a nice, well brought up little girl I think I'd do anything in the world for you."

She promised that too. In fact, by the time she finally left the office and was on her way uptown, late for an engagement she had with Horace Bayne, she was alarmed to remember how many things she had promised—not only to stay until he came back but to write to him every day, a long report of just what had happened in the family and what her impressions of it were.

"Not letters," he had said, "because I shan't answer them; but reports—reports on my family, as I am going to make a report on this mine."

They were to be typewritten. He had no intention of struggling with any woman's handwriting, though Augusta murmured that hers was considered very legible.

It was not her custom to take a definite step like this without consulting Horace—not so much because Horace insisted on it as because she thought highly of his opinion. She was astonished now, as in the Subway she thought over the interview, to find how little she had been thinking of Horace. They had been engaged for something over two years, one of those comfortable engagements, which until recently had had no prospects of marriage.

The Rutland College Club is almost deserted in summer. As she ran upstairs to the library, where she was to meet Horace, she glanced at her watch and saw to her regret that he must have been waiting almost an hour, for he was punctual, and usually arrived a little ahead of the hour. She was sorry—such a busy man; but he would understand—she would explain——

He rose from a deep chair as she entered—a serious young man whom everyone trusted at first sight. She saw he looked a little more serious than usual, and her sense of guilt made her attribute this seriousness to her own fault. She began to explain quickly and with unaccustomed vivacity. She sketched the interview—Mr. Wood—his office—the promise—the letters—the turquoise. Horace kept getting more and more solemn, although it seemed to her that she made a very good story of it—more amusing perhaps than the reality had been.

"Isn't it exciting?" she said. "I'm going down on Thursday, under this contract, to stay two months."

"No, you're not," said Horace.

She stared at him. He had never spoken like that in all the years she had known him.

"What do you mean, dear?" she said rather reprovingly.

"You were so busy telling me about this Adonis you're going to work for you did not stop to consider that I might have some news of my own. I've landed that job in Canada, and I'm going there on Friday and you're going with me. You're going to marry me the day after tomorrow and start north on Friday."

She stared at him, many emotions succeeding each other on her face. She had given her word—her most solemn word. She could hear Wood's quiet voice asserting his confidence in her. "I know I can depend on you; if you give me your word I know you'll keep it." She could not break it. She said this, expecting that Horace would admire her for her dependability—would at least agree with her that she was doing right. But instead he looked at her with a smoldering expression, and when she had finished he broke out. In fact he made her a scene of jealousy—the first he had ever made—but none the worse for that. For a beginner Horace showed a good deal of talent. He accused her openly of having fallen in love with this fellow; she wasn't a girl to do anything as silly as that except under a hypnotic influence. People did fall in love at first sight. There were Romeo and Juliet;

Shakespeare was a fairly wise guy—these letters every day—why, if she wrote to him, Horace, once a week he was lucky—but every day to this man. And jewels and money—no, not much!

Jealousy, which is popularly supposed to be an erratic and fantastic emotion, is often founded on the soundest intuition. Augusta found herself hampered in defending herself by a certain inner doubt; and her silence enabled Horace to work himself up to such a pitch that he issued an ultimatum—a dangerous thing to do. She would either marry him and go to Canada with him, or else everything was over between them.

It was a terrible situation for Augusta. On the one hand, her spoken word, given to a person whose good opinion she greatly desired, and on the other, her sincere love of Horace, increased by the decisive stand he was taking; for it is unfortunately true that if you do not hate a person for making a scene you love him more.

Perhaps Horace saw this. In any case, he would not retreat an inch. This was the situation when the door of the library opened and in came Augusta's friend and classmate, Pearl Leavitt, with whom she had an engagement for luncheon—only in the general strain and excitement of the morning she had entirely forgotten the fact.

Pearl, like Augusta herself, was too much occupied with her own mood to notice that a mood was already waiting for her. It seemed to her that Augusta and Horace were just sitting there as usual, without much to say to each other. She had been looking for a job all the morning, and all the day before, and was discovering that beauty may find it as hard to get a job as it had been to keep one.

"Hullo, Gussie! Hullo, Horrie!" she said, striding in, full of her own troubles. "I think men are just terrible."

"You must have changed a lot," said Bayne, who was in no humor to let anything pass.

He had known Pearl since her freshman year at Rutland, and was accustomed to seeing her surrounded by a flock of the condemned sex, whose attentions had never seemed unwelcome.

"Yes, I've changed," said Pearl. "You see, I've worked for men—at least I've tried to. I've been trying to all morning. If they kept turning you down because you were lame or marked with smallpox they'd feel ashamed, but if they turn you down because they think you're good-looking——" Miss Leavitt here interrupted her narrative to give a grinning representation of the speaker. "'Forgive my speaking plainly, but you are too good-looking for office work.' Doesn't it occur to them that even good-looking people must eat? And they are so smug and pleased with themselves. Well, here I am with two weeks' salary between me and starvation—all on account of my looks. I believe I'll go and teach in a convent, where there are not any men to be rendered hysterical by my appearance."

And she gave a terrible glance at Horace, and then feeling she had been too severe she beamed at him—beaming at Horace was perfectly safe—and added, "I've always liked you, Horrie; but I have no use for your sex—especially as employers; they are too emotional."

"And what would you say, Pearl," said Horace in a deadly impartial tone, "if a man offered you a job, and in the first interview told his life's story, asked you to write to him every day and promised you jewels if you stayed on the job until he got back—what would you say?"

"I wouldn't say a word," answered Pearl. "I'd take to the tall timber. I know that kind."

"You are both absolutely ridiculous," said Augusta haughtily.

"You are absolutely right," said Horace.

"You don't mean to say that someone has been trying to wangle Augusta away from you, Horace?" asked Pearl, generously abandoning all interest in her own problems for the moment.

The two others said no and yes simultaneously, and began to pour out the story. Augusta's point was that Horace did not respect her business honor or else he would not ask her to break—Horace's point was that Augusta did not really love him or she wouldn't think up all these excuses—she'd marry him as he asked her to do. Ah, but he hadn't had any idea of getting married until he heard that she was going to take this place! He had—he had—he had come there to tell her, only she had been so excited about this other man —— Nonsense, the trouble with Horace was that he was jealous. No, he was not at all jealous, but if he were he had good reason to be—writing to a man every day, and accepting jewels ——

Pearl kept looking from one to the other, deeply interested. In the first pause—which did not come for a long time—she said gravely, "How is it, Gussie? Do you really want to marry Horace?"

She said it very nicely, but on her expressive face was written the thought that she herself could not see how anyone could want to marry him.

"I do, I do," answered Augusta rather tearfully; "but how can I when I've given my word?"

"I'll tell you how you can," said Pearl. "You marry him and disappear into the wilds of Canada, and I'll take your place with the Conway family."

They stared at each other like people waiting for the sound of an explosion. They were trying to think of obstacles.

"Except," said Pearl, "that I'm not efficient like you, and not very good at mathematics."

"You were efficient in the way you ran the junior ball," said Augusta. "Everyone said——"

A spasm of amusement crossed Pearl's face.

"Did I never tell you about that?" she said. "I vamped the senior at Amherst who had run theirs, and he not only gave me all the dope but he did most of my work. I was a mine of information. But that isn't efficiency."

"I disagree with you," said Augusta.

The more she thought of this idea, the more it seemed to her perfect. There had always been a kind of magic about Pearl, and wasn't magic the highest form of human efficiency? It was not breaking one's word to substitute a better article than that contracted for. To send Pearl in her place would be keeping her word doubly. She saw Pearl charming Antonia, dazzling the boy, setting all the Conway household to rights by ways peculiarly her own.

"But perhaps they won't want Pearl," said Horace. "I mean——"

"They won't have any choice," said the two girls together.

"But I mean," reiterated Horace, "that no one would want a governess who looked like Pearl."

Then the storm broke over his head. What? Wouldn't he even let her be a governess? Did he want her just to starve? Would he tell her what she could do? Starve perhaps—just starve—all men were alike. Again Pearl began to stride up and down the room, flicking the front of her small black hat with her forefinger until finally it fell off and rolled on the floor like an old-fashioned cannon ball. If Horace had spoken from motives of diplomacy he could not have done better for himself. His objection made the two girls a unit for the plan. It just showed, Pearl explained, that if Horace, who had known her all these years, really considered her looks an obstacle to her taking a place even as a governess, why, it was hopeless to suppose that she could ever get another job.

At length they sent him away—he had a business engagement of his own for lunch—and they settled down quietly to discuss the details of the plan over one of the small bare gray wood tables of the club's dining room. Ordinarily they would have spent most of their time complaining about the club luncheon, which consisted largely of loose leaves of lettuce and dabs of various kinds of sauces; but now they were so interested that they were hardly conscious of what they put into their mouths.

Of course, Pearl would be obliged to go in the character of Miss Exeter. Mr. Wood would undoubtedly have given some description of the governess' personal appearance when he telephoned his sister, as he had said he meant to do. But Augusta was not alarmed by this idea. Men were so queer about women's looks that Mrs. Conway would say, "Isn't that like a man, not even to know a great beauty when he sees one?" As to the daily letter, how fortunate that he had insisted it should be typewritten. Anyone could sign Augusta Exeter to a man who had seen her signature only once.

"I hope you won't be found out; I don't see how you can be," said Augusta.

"I can't see that it matters much if I am," answered Pearl. "I'll try to put it off, anyhow, until they have become attached to me for myself." And then suddenly falling back in her chair, she stared at her friend with opened eyes. "My dear, I can't do it! How could I have forgotten? I can't leave Alfred!"

Alfred was not a beautiful young lover, as her tone of lingering affection might have seemed to indicate, but a peculiarly ugly black-and-white cat—black where he ought to have been white, and vice versa—that is to say, black round one eye, which made him look dissipated, and black about the nose, which made him look dirty. Also he had lost one paw. Pearl had rescued him from a band of boys in an alley and cherished him with a steady maternal affection.

"Oh, Alfred," said Augusta, as if this did not make much difference.

This was not only wrong in tone but she had failed to say the thing Pearl wanted her to say, namely, that Mrs. Conway would be delighted if the new governess brought her pet cat with her. Pearl explained that Alfred was really no trouble in the house—he slept all day and caught mice at night—except one night he did tumble all the way downstairs on account of his paw.

"And you'd be surprised, Gussie," said Pearl, her whole generous face lighting up with admiration; "that cat—that little creature made a noise like an elephant falling, he's so solid."

But Augusta, who was not so easily moved to admiration as Pearl, was not at all moved now.

"I can't see," she observed coldly, "what it is you see in Alfred that makes you love him so."

Pearl, who had really a nice nature, wasn't angry.

"It isn't exactly that I love him so much," she answered. "But I feel so sorry for him; and when I feel sorry for anyone they to a certain extent own me. I feel as if I could never make up to them for the way life has treated them. I feel that way to Alfred—about his paw, you know."

"You didn't feel that way to the man who cried in the Encyclopedia."

"I should say not," answered Pearl. "No, I can't pity him. He was such a poor sport about it. Men are poor sports where women are concerned—even Horace. If you had asked him to break his word because you had had a brain storm he'd have been shocked."

"He'd have been immensely flattered," said Augusta reflectively.

"But he thinks it's absolutely all right for him to break up all your business arrangements because he goes off halfcocked with a fantastic idea that you've fallen in love with a man you merely want to work for."

Augusta thought a minute and then she said, "It wasn't quite so fantastic as you think, Pearl. I was attracted by Mr. Wood. I might have fallen in love with him if I had been brought into contact with him much more. Oh, Pearl, haven't you ever felt a sudden charm like that?"

Pearl shook her head: She could not say,—perhaps she did not really herself understand why such emotions were forbidden to her, but the true reason was that if her speaking countenance had ever turned upon a man with that thought in mind the next instant her lovely nose would have been buried in a tweed lapel or grating against a stiff collar.

"You know," Augusta went on, "that I really love Horace; and Mr. Wood took no interest in me, except as a governess for his nieces; but have you never said to yourself, 'There is the type of man whom I could have loved madly if only things had been different'?"

Again Pearl's head wagged. Then she said, "Describe my employer to me."

"Well," Augusta began solemnly, "he has a smooth brown face out of which look two bright-blue eyes like a Chinaman."

Pearl scowled.

"But Chinamen don't have blue eyes," she objected.

"No more they do. Why did I keep thinking of China then? China-blue, perhaps, or maybe the way they are set. I think there is an angle—a little up at the corners. Then his shoulders are broad, or his waist is awfully thin, because his coat falls in that loose nice way, like the English officers who came to lecture at college."

"Mercy," said Pearl, "what things you notice!"

"And he's very direct, and not at all afraid of saying what has to be said. And he doesn't lecture you about women's intuition or how he made his business success or any of those things that men always do talk about when they offer you a job. And oh, it rings in my ears the way he said as we parted, 'If you give me your word I know I can trust you to keep it,' or something like that."

And at this moment the housekeeper of the club came into the dining room, nominally to see that luncheon was being properly served, but actually, as she soon explained, because the club was so lonely in summer, and her little dog had been killed by an automobile the week before. Pearl was, of course, immensely sympathetic about this loss; and Augusta, with a flash of efficiency, suggested that Alfred could live at the club for the two months Pearl was away, and the housekeeper greeted the idea with enthusiasm.

And so, the last obstacle being removed, these two efficient women went upstairs to the library and, sitting side by side, with the black notebook between them, worked the whole thing out, as in their college days they had so often worked up an examination. All the facts that Wood had spread out for Augusta, Augusta now spread out for Pearl—the salary, the bonus, the characters of those involved, the results which Mr. Wood especially wished to see accomplished: That Antonia should be made clean and neat and dressed like a normal little girl; that Durland should be taught algebra thoroughly and made to stop smoking, though that would be difficult; that Mrs. Conway should not be worried by her former husband, and certainly prevented from lending him money.

"And there is his address in Mexico, and you're to write every day. That's the most important thing of all—to write every day."

Pearl took the notebook and put it into her pocketbook.

"And how often does he write to me?" she inquired.

Augusta smiled.

"He never does—he never answers. I suppose it's the first time in your life, Pearl, you ever wrote to a man who did not answer your letters."

"I rather like the idea," said Pearl.

They were interrupted by a telegram being brought in and given to Augusta. She opened it.

"It's from Mr. Wood," she said; and added with surprise, "It seems to be about you."

"About me?"

"No," said Augusta with relief, "I read it wrong. It's about Mrs. Conway's jewels. He told me she had a string of priceless pearls that her husband gave her when they were first married.

"The message says, 'Please see that pearls are kept in safe on account of recent Long Island burglaries.'" She gave the yellow sheet to her friend. "Keep that," she said, "and be sure to mention in your first report that you have received it. That will make absolutely sure that you're me."

"You ought to say 'you're I' if you are going to be a governess," said Pearl.

"But I'm not," said Augusta.

CHAPTER TWO

The following Thursday afternoon Pearl stepped from the fast train to the platform of the Southampton station. Since the train reached Quogue she had been agreeably aware of the damp saltness in the air, which comes only from proximity to the open ocean. But now, on the platform, she smelled nothing but the fumes of innumerable exhausts, saw nothing but masses of automobiles crowding toward the station like a flock of parti-colored elephants. She stood dazed for a minute by the noise of self-starters and the crowd of arrivals, until, darting in and out under the elbows of chauffeurs and passengers, she saw a little bareheaded, barefooted figure in a dirty white dress edged with the finest Valenciennes lace. Pearl felt an instant conviction that this was her future charge.

"Antonia," she said in her deep voice, and the child made a rush for her.

"Are you Miss Exeter?" she exclaimed, and she gave a little boyish shake to her head. "I must say I think you are much more than pleasing. My mother said you'd be much less. She drew me a picture of what she thought you'd look like. Mother doesn't draw very well. I'm glad you're not like that. If I'd taken that as a guide I'd never have found you at all."

She beckoned to a large green touring car, and having arranged about Pearl's trunk and seen the bags put into the car, she herself sank beside Pearl on the wide back seat, while to steady herself on the slippery leather she raised one leg and clutched the back of the front seat with her bare flexible toes.

"How do you like Southampton?" she said.

If they had gone down the main street Pearl would have seen some old gray-shingled houses and elm trees that she would have honestly admired but they had turned eastward and were now driving down a perfectly straight road at the end of which, through a dip in the dunes, the deep blue of the afternoon sea could be seen. The country was flat in every direction except the north, where a wooded rise in the ground cut off the horizon. To be candid, Pearl did not greatly admire the prospect, but she said tactfully, "I love the sea."

"Can you swim?"

"Yes."

"Can you play tennis?"

"Yes."

"Can you drive a car?"

"No."

"Good!" said the child with her friendly smile. "I'm glad I've found something you can't do. Beckett," she said, leaning forward and shouting in the ear of the chauffeur, "I mean to teach Miss Exeter to drive."

"Maybe it'd be as well to learn yourself first, miss," said the man coldly.

Antonia sighed.

"Beckett's cross," she said, "because I bent the fender coming up. My legs are too short to reach the foot brake in a hurry. Beckett knows that, but he doesn't make allowances."

"Is it safe for you to drive, then?" asked Pearl.

"Well, if you ask me, no," said Antonia candidly; "but as long as mother lets me do it, of course I'm going to. I wonder if you're going to like us. I don't see how anyone could like Dolly."

"What's the matter with Dolly?"

"Oh, about everything," answered Antonia. "I'll tell you the kind of person she is: If you forget something she asks you to do she treats you as if you were a moron to have forgotten it, and if she forgets something you ask her to do she treats you as if you were a moron to have asked her to do it."

"There must be something to be said for her," Pearl suggested.

Antonia considered the question. She was, as her uncle had said, the justest of created beings.

"I suppose there must be, but I don't know what it is. Then there's Durland—he's great—only he doesn't notice me much. I wish I were a boy. I want to wear trousers and be free."

"You seem to me pretty fairly free."

Antonia laughed.

"That's funny," she said. "I mean it's funny that you said that exactly the way Uncle Anthony talks—that gentle tone that makes you feel like nothing at all. Do you like Uncle Anthony? Do you think he's handsome?"

"Yes, indeed I do," answered Pearl, with the modest enthusiasm which she thought under the circumstances Augusta would have allowed herself.

"So do I," said Antonia. "So does Miss Wellington, whose mother has the house next us. She took it before she knew Uncle Anthony was going to be away all summer—at least that's what mother and I think. Miss Wellington told me she thought him handsome and she said 'And you can tell him I said so,' but I didn't—for rather a spiteful reason; I thought she wanted me to."

"It sounds that way to me, too," said Pearl.

"I'm glad you like him," Antonia went on. "He likes you too. He telephoned mother about you. He said he had found a pearl—wasn't that funny?" It was funnier than Antonia knew. "So now mother always speaks of you as the priceless pearl. Mother's rather amusing, like that. He said you were not so much on looks—just pleasing, he said. But I think you are perfectly beautiful. Do you think you're beautiful, Miss Exeter?"

This was the first crisis. Pearl knew that if she said no Antonia would distrust her honesty, and if she said yes it might be used against her. So she compromised.

"I'll answer that question the day I leave," she said.

"I'll tell you something funny about that," said Antonia. "Perhaps I oughtn't to, but I'm going to. Uncle Anthony made mother promise not to send you away until he came back, no matter what happened; but mother says she knows a way to get round that if the worst comes to the worst. You see, I don't want to hurt your feelings; but we all felt it was rather hard on us to have a governess at all in summer. Mother thinks it's hard too. She says it's just one of Uncle Anthony's ideas. She says a man can't take an interest in anything unless he thinks he's running it. So she just lets him think he runs the family, and then when he's away she does what she thinks best. This is our gate now. What do you think of the house? We only rent it. There's Durland going in for a swim before dinner. I wonder if he'd wait for us. Durland! Durland!"

It was quite extraordinary the volume of sound that could issue from so small a person as Antonia. She sprang out of the car over the closed door and ran round the house toward the ocean, while Pearl entered the front door alone.

A slim, gray-haired figure in delft blue came out of a neighboring room and said "Good heavens, you are not Miss Exeter, are you?"

Pearl smiled her most winning smile.

"Won't I do?" she said.

But merriment did not seem quite in order. Mrs. Conway's manners were perfect, but she was not going to begin by being any more friendly than she could help.

She answered politely, "Oh, perfectly, I feel sure. Only you do not look quite as my brother's description led me to expect; but then men are not very good at describing women."

Her hair, prematurely gray, gave more the effect of powder. Her brows were arched so much that she seemed to be looking up from under a thatch. They were blue eyes; not quite China blue, as Pearl had heard the family eyes described; they were sad, appealing eyes, which kept veiling themselves in an effort to seem dignified and remote. Yes, Pearl thought, there was something pathetic about Mrs. Conway—something that made her feel just a little bit as Alfred's lost paw made her feel; so she beamed gently down upon her new employer while that lady continued:

"I don't see how Antonia ever found you—from his account. Fortunately the child is wonderfully quick or you would be waiting at the station still. Where is she, by the way?"

Pearl explained that she had dashed down to the beach to ask her brother to wait for them, and would it be all right if she went swimming too? Over Mrs. Conway's shoulder Pearl could catch a glimpse of the piazza, and beyond that the faultless blue rim of the horizon; and as she talked she could hear close by the thud and hiss as a wave went up the beach. She longed to be in the water.

"Oh, yes, go if you want to," said Mrs. Conway. She was not exactly cordial. Gentle, friendly people like Edna Conway always go too far when they try to be cold; they have no experience in the rôle. "But try not to keep them waiting too long. My children hate to be kept waiting."

"I do myself," answered Pearl gayly.

"Really?" said Mrs. Conway, and the arched eyebrows went up under the gray thatch.

Pearl saw she had said the wrong thing; but whether it was wrong for a governess to dislike being kept waiting, or presumptuous to put herself into the same interesting group as the Conway children, she had no idea. She did not much care either. The smooth blue sea was waiting for her, and she went springing upstairs, slinging off a string of beads—translucent pearl-gray glass, the color of her eyes—and thinking to herself that it was a mercy she had had sense enough to put her bathing dress in her bag. She tore it out from the lower layers so violently that shoes and brushes flew into the air like stones from a volcano; and in a surprisingly short time she was running through the deserted sitting room, out across the piazza, down the steep wooden steps to the beach.

At the edge of the water Durland was standing with his back to her. Although he was a thin boy of fifteen in a striped red-and-blue bathing suit, he was standing with one knee advanced, his hand on his hip and a cigarette dangling from his lip, as if he were the late King Edward VII at Homburg. Beside him, Antonia was digging a hole like a dog—possibly her sleeping hole for the evening—and talking all the time. She was talking about Miss Exeter.

Durland was deeply opposed to the idea of Miss Exeter. In the first place he was opposed to women, as a prisoner is opposed to stone walls. He was surrounded by them, dominated by them. His mother, his mother's maid, who had been with them forever, his sister Dorothy—they all bullied him and cut him off from his fellow men. Sometimes, with disgust, he heard himself using the feminized vocabulary of the women about him, and though he was as masculine as possible—smoked and everything—he could not shake off their influence. Then he hated governesses as representing that most emasculated form of that most emasculated thing—learning. His friends had already made fun of him about it. It had been said on the beach, "I hear they're getting a governess to keep you in order, Durlie." He had decided to make it clear that he had nothing to do with the woman. He doubted if he even allowed her to teach him algebra, though as a matter of fact he wanted to pass his examination. And then, last but not least of his reasons, he felt opposed to anything that Antonia so wildly recommended, because that was one way of keeping her in the complete subjection to him in which she lived.

So while she chattered of Miss Exeter and her beauty and her youngness and the sort of niceness of the way in which she looked at you, he stood gazing out to sea as if the best he could do for his little sister was just not to hear her at all.

Then Antonia cried "Here she is!" and executed a four-footed leap on finger tips and toes; and then Durland was aware of a circular motion of white arms and long white legs whirling past his shoulder, and the new governess had plunged into the Atlantic.

This really wouldn't do at all—governess doing hand-springs. It looked peculiar, and yet it did pique the curiosity. He sauntered a step nearer with a slow, sophisticated, loose-kneed walk. Miss Exeter and Antonia were behaving foolishly, and noisily, too—splashing each other and laughing. He himself went in as if the object of a swim were not to disturb one unnecessary drop of water. He swam a stroke or two under the surface, and coming up out of a wave found himself face to face with Pearl. The wonderful radiance of those gray eyes came to rest on his; and his heart melted within him like a pat of butter. It wasn't just her beauty though that would probably have been enough; but it was the immense, generous friendliness toward all the world when the world would allow her to be friendly that warmed and comforted his young spirit. He gazed at her, and suddenly the gaze was cut short by Pearl's decision to stand on her head. Two white feet clapped together in front of Durland's nose.

If she had been less beautiful he would have said to himself that she really did not know how to behave. As it was, he thought that she would certainly lay herself open to unkind criticism. He wanted to protect her, and he was not without tact. He said, when she came to the surface, blinking the water from her long, matted eyelashes, "It's nice to have our own beach, isn't it?—to be able to do what we like—stand on our heads or anything without being talked about."

She did not seem to get it at all.

"Let's swim out," she said, and laid her ear upon the face of the sea as if she were a baby listening to the ticking of a watch. He swam beside her, looking into her face, and she gave him a friendly little beam every now and then. It was wonderful to be under no necessity of suppressing her cheerful kindness of heart. "Let it do its deadly work" was her feeling.

They had a good long swim, and when they came in were met by Mrs. Conway at the head of the steps. She was dressed for dinner in a faint pink tea gown with pearls.

She said civilly, but all on one note, "Dinner is ready, Miss Exeter."

Yes, she who had so often waited uncomplainingly for hours for her children, pretending that the clocks were wrong, or the dinner hour changed, or that the mistake had been hers, was now feeling outraged at being obliged to wait ten minutes for this governess her brother had so obstinately insisted on engaging.

"Oh, I won't be a minute, Mrs. Conway," said Pearl, feeling genuinely sorry to have inconvenienced anyone, but not feeling at all guilty as Mrs. Conway wanted her to feel.

"Yes, I do hope you'll contrive not to be very long," she said, and could not understand the cause for a dark look her son gave her as he pursued his shivering way upstairs.

She went into the sitting room, where her daughter Dorothy was already waiting. It was not a miracle that Dolly was ready on time, but a phenomenon to be explained by the fact that she had a bridge engagement immediately after dinner.

She was a pretty, round-faced girl, rather like her mother, except that her hair was still a natural light brown, and her eyes were brown too. She did not raise her head, as her mother entered, from the fashion paper which she was languidly studying.

"Not a very promising beginning, is it?" said Mrs. Conway. She knew Dolly would be annoyed and she wished to cut herself off completely from the guilty one. "Do you suppose she's going to keep us waiting for dinner half an hour every evening?"

Dolly bent her head to examine a picture of an ermine wrap.

"Oh, well, mother," she said, "what can you expect if you give in to every whim of Uncle Anthony's?"

Mrs. Conway made a pathetic little grimace—pathetic because it was so obviously intended to win Dolly to her side—to make the girl feel that she and her mother had a secret alliance against the world at large.

"You'll find, my dear," she said, "that in dealing with men it's easier to yield at the moment and find a way out at leisure."

But Dolly, who had not even looked up long enough to see the grimace, answered with a bitter little laugh, "It may be easier for you, but not for us. We have to suffer. That's the trouble with you, mother—you think of no one in the world but yourself."

Her mother did not answer—she could not. Tears rose in her blue eyes. She had enormous capacity for being hurt. Strangely enough, there was something in her that drove those she loved to say exactly the thing that would hurt her most. It had always been so with her husband, and now it was so with her children.

A misplaced fortitude always led her to hide the fact that she was hurt.

She said now with false gayety, "Well, my dear, I hope some day you will find someone who loves you even better than I do, then."

"I'm sure I hope so," said Dolly, turning the page.

Her manner suggested that if she could not do that much her life would indeed be a failure.

Mrs. Conway stepped out on the piazza. That was the way—you gave up your life to making your children happy, to shielding them from grief and anxiety, and then they blamed you and hurt you horribly for something that was not at all your fault. She felt a moment of resentment toward her brother. Why had Anthony insisted on this silly plan? She had been too considerate of Anthony's feelings; she ought to have refused to have a governess at all. It was much wiser in this world to be stern and cruel. She decided to be stern and to begin with Miss Exeter, who entered the sitting room at this moment. She was wearing a plain cream-colored dress out of which her lovely head—all brown and rose color and gold—seemed strangely bright colored.

"I suppose you're Dolly," she said in her deep warm voice, and held out an open hand.

Dolly, like most young people, estimated beauty as the best of gifts. She might have been almost as much captured by Pearl's as her brother had been, except that her ego was taken up with the outrage of her being kept waiting—she, the most important person in the house, who had taken the trouble not only to order dinner on time but—what did not always happen—to be on time herself.

She rose, and allowing a limp hand to pass rapidly through Miss Exeter's, she said, "Do let's go in to dinner, mother."

"Yes, indeed," said her mother, coming in rapidly from the piazza. "We dine at eight, Miss Exeter. Another evening I'm sure you will be on time."

This was not perhaps a very terrible beginning to a régime of sternness; but to Durland, just getting down, it appeared one of the most disgusting exhibitions of slave driving that he had ever heard.

"It is entirely my fault that we are late," he said, giving his mother a steady, brave look.

She answered irrelevantly, "Why, Durland, how nice you look! Are you going anywhere this evening?"

"Very likely," he answered coldly. He thought to himself, "Why must she give Miss Exeter the impression that I look like a cowboy generally?" He was of course going nowhere.

So, having completely alienated her two elder children—Antonia had early supper by herself—Mrs. Conway found herself obliged to direct her conversation to the interloper. She had her revenge, if she had only known it, by talking about her brother, questioning Miss Exeter about him. Had he seemed very much rushed? Did he say anything about his golf clubs? Wasn't it a delightful office? Wonderful! So cool in summer.

Pearl hazarded that the harbor was very beautiful, and learned that Mr. Wood's office looked north—up the Hudson. She must be careful.

Durland inquired with a friendly grin whether Uncle Anthony had frightened her to death.

"Frightened me?" said Pearl, trying to gain time.

"Some people are awfully afraid of him."

"Naughty little boys are," said Dolly.

It always annoyed her to see her brother sitting at the foot of the dinner table. They had fought about it for five years—whether she as eldest child or he as the only man in the house ought to occupy this place of honor.

"I'm not afraid of him," said Durland.

"Oh, are you a naughty little boy?" said Dolly, laughing in an irritating way.

Mrs. Conway, to avert war, began talking about the day's schedule—the problem of how to work in a few lessons without interfering with any of the more important pleasures of her children.

"Antonia first, I think. Wouldn't that be your idea, Dolly—Antonia at half past nine? Dolly and Durland sometimes sleep rather late—so good for them, I think—but Antonia is up early. She reads sometimes from five o'clock. She reads a great deal—everything."

"Quite the little genius, according to mother," said Dolly.

"She is clever," answered Mrs. Conway passionately. "I don't know why you two are always so disagreeable about your little sister."

"Because you spoil her so, mother," said Dolly.

"Because she's so dirty, mother," said Durland.

Mrs. Conway made this attack a means of aligning herself with her children against the governess.

"Oh, well," she said, "that is all going to be changed now. Miss Exeter is going to make us all over. Antonia is to be clean and tidy, though why in the world your uncle thinks it desirable for a child of eleven to think of nothing but clothes I can't see. And Durland is to be made into a mathematician. I suppose I'm very ignorant, but I never could see what good algebra does a person—all about greyhounds leaping after hares, and men doing pieces of work at seventy-five cents a day. I wish I could find some like that. Poor Durland, like so many people with a creative turn of mind, simply cannot do mathematics."

"More people than creative geniuses are poor at mathematics," said Pearl genially; and Durland, afraid that she would identify him with his mother in this ridiculous point of view, looked into those pools of gray light and said modestly that he was just a dub at problems.

"Then at half past eleven," Mrs. Conway went on, "you'll be free to take Antonia to the beach—the public beach, where she likes to get a swim and see her little friends."

"Fight a round or two with her little enemies," said her brother.

"She's only fought once this summer," said his mother. "And I for one think she was perfectly right. Maud is the most annoying child—ugly and impertinent like her mother, and very badly brought up."

"Well, that's not a patch on what they think about Antonia," said Durland, and he turned to Miss Exeter. "Gee, it was great! This Maud child said something rude about Antonia's bare feet, and she sailed in and landed her one on the jaw; and they fought so that the nurses and governesses all ran screaming away and the life-saving men had to come in and separate them."

Mrs. Conway hated this story about her youngest child.

She rose from table in order to interrupt it, observing that Durland needn't worry, as now they were all going to be made perfect.

Pearl on the whole felt encouraged. Augusta, with all her efficiency, could not have swung this job, she thought. It required a solid, almost irrational good temper, which Augusta did not possess. Mrs. Conway would have rendered Augusta acid and powerless in one evening. Pearl was not so efficient in certain ways, but she had good temper and a robust will.

She and Durland went into the sitting room while Mrs. Conway was getting Dolly off to her bridge party. Durland did what, alas, men have been doing for many centuries—he attempted to impress the object of his affection by doing one of the things most certain to alienate her. He stood before her, lighting a cigarette, shaking the match deliberately in the air, his legs rather wide apart. Pearl, who had sunk into a nice deep chair, sprang up and put her hand on his shoulder.

"Oh, don't smoke," she said.

Hundreds of women had said that to him. Even the lovely Caroline Temple—his former love—had said that her parents had forbidden her to have him at the house on account of his smoking; such a bad example.

"Caroline," he had said quietly, "I simply do openly what all the others do secretly."

He had not wavered about it. Neither had her parents. He and Caroline met at the tennis club and at the beach—no longer at her house. But he had never thought of changing his habits. His cigarette was to him what a car is to a theatrical star—a symbol of greatness. He was firm now, even under the pleading of a new idol.

"I'm afraid I can't give it up," he said. "I'm afraid it has too much of a grip on me for that."

He frowned as one who, looking inward, saw nothing but vice and ruin. He was disappointed to find that she just let it drop—as if she were not vitally interested in saving him. But before he had time to commit the natural mistake of asking her why she did not rescue him from his worse self, his mother came back into the room.

Her first words were, "Do you think that a good picture of my brother?"

Something mocking and teasing in her tone unnerved Pearl a little; so that instead of following the direction of Mrs. Conway's eyes she said rather wildly, "Where?"

Durland came to her rescue by politely giving her a large silver frame in which was the photograph of a man she was prepared to admire, and so she did admire him—so much that something tense was apparent as she gazed into those China-blue eyes, which looked—if one had not had private information—as if they were brown.

Mrs. Conway watched with sly amusement. The mocking quality in her question had not arisen, as Pearl half feared, from any doubt as to the new governess' identity, but rather from the suspicion that there was more between her brother and this lovely creature than had been confessed. Like many gentle sweet people, Edna Conway was extremely suspicious; her mind ran rapidly over a situation, examining though not necessarily believing all the darkest possibilities. She did not actually suspect her brother of finding a safe home for a dangerous girl during his absence, but she did say to herself—perhaps not unnaturally, "There's more in this than meets the eye."

A voice from the piazza called, "Did Anthony's pearl arrive?" And a woman in evening dress entered.

"Yes, Cora, this is she," said Mrs. Conway, and she added with a certain hint of malice, "You ought to know each other—both so consecrated to doing whatever Anthony wants done. Miss Exeter, Miss Wellington."

Miss Wellington's emotions were clearly written on her face. She had been in love with Anthony ever since he succeeded. This which sounds like a paradox was the simple truth. To her, success was not necessarily financial—though Wood's had had this agreeable aspect—but importance and preëminence were to her as essential elements in male attraction as feminine beauty is to most men. When she was eighteen and Anthony still in the School of Mines there had been sentimental scenes which had left her cold. She occasionally referred to them as "the time when you thought you wanted to marry me," and he did not contradict her. He had thought he did. He still admired her—she was elegant in appearance, beautifully dressed, competent in all the practical aspects of life. If she had married someone else he would have said to her, "Your marriage was a great blow to me, Cora. I had always fancied that some day you and I———" But he never would have said it until after she was safely married.

She had, however, no intention of marrying anyone else—for the simple reason that Anthony was by far the most attractive man of importance that she knew. Her feelings on discovering Pearl—the young person she had heard described as being of merely pleasing appearance—to be an exuberant beauty, and discovering her, moreover, staring sentimentally at Anthony's picture, were not suspicions; she had the conviction of disaster. She couldn't be cordial; and, Pearl, who had the kind of sensitiveness that comes from generosity, not from egotism, saw that the moment had come for her to go upstairs and write her first letter to the man whose face she liked so much.

She had always been a poor correspondent. She had never enjoyed writing before, but now the idea of pouring herself out—or rather not herself, but her observation of a situation in which he was vitally interested—delighted her. All of us, it has been said, can write well if we have something interesting to say. What Pearl had to say could not fail to be interesting to the man she was writing to. There was no motive for caution. At last she had found a man with whom she could be candid and natural. Late into the night the sound of a portable typewriter could be heard ticking from the room of the new governess.

It was not easy to put a routine into operation in the Conway household. At half past nine, the hour set for Antonia's lessons, Antonia was nowhere to be found. Pearl at last ventured to tap at Mrs. Conway's bedroom door. Mrs. Conway was sitting up in bed, in white satin and yellow lace, with her breakfast tray on her lap.

In response to the news that her youngest child was missing, she answered, "She's probably gone crabbing. I'm afraid that if you want to do lessons in summer you will have to get up a little earlier. She was out of the house by seven, I dare say." And she smiled maliciously.

Pearl saw that coöperation was unlikely, hostility probable, and withdrew.

Durland, her second pupil, presented himself a little ahead of time. He came downstairs at ten, drank a cup of black coffee and ate a peach. He was recklessly wearing his last pair of clean white trousers. He was paler and more like a young bird than usual. He, too, had his problems.

While willing to oblige Miss Exeter in every particular, while eager to help her and make her appear a worker of miracles, her mere proximity prevented his mind from functioning at all. Do what she could, her efforts to get him thinking about the problem of three men, A, B and C, who, working together, could do a piece of work in three days, was like trying to crank a dead automobile. She tried beaming upon him, she tried being severe; either way his intense emotion flooded his mental processes.

She thought, "I've solved worse problems than this, but I'm sure I don't know what to do."

He himself gave her the clew. She had explained for the third time that if you let x equal the number of days that it took A, working alone—when he interrupted her. He was sitting beside her, leaning his head on his hand and staring at her in a maze of admiration.

Suddenly he said, "Do you like teaching, Miss Exeter?"

"I like teaching girls," she answered with a quick inspiration.

He drove his unwilling intelligence to take in this incredible statement.

"Girls," he said, opening his honest blue eyes and wrinkling his forehead. "Why girls?"

"They're so much cleverer than boys."

She tossed it off as if were a well-known and generally admitted fact. He was gentle with her.

"People think just the opposite," he said.

"Men do."

"I think you're wrong about that, really," Durland said. "I think anyone—even a very just man like Uncle Anthony—would say that women can't think, at least not like men."

"Would he, indeed?" said Pearl. "Well, I don't know him; but he may be the kind of man who prefers inferior people of both sexes."

Durland, unable to believe she really thought this, looked wistfully into her face for a sign of relenting.

"Of course," he said, "you are very unusual. You must not judge other women by yourself."

"I was fifteenth in my class," said Pearl. "Quite stupid compared to the others; but even I never had any trouble with algebra. I put my mind on it. That's the trouble with boys—they're so scattered."

This was cruel, considering who had scattered him; but like many cruelties it worked.

As the hour finished, Dolly came downstairs and said, without looking at anyone, that she herself was going immediately in the motor to Shinnecock for her golf lesson and could not delay an instant; but if Antonia were there and ready there was no objection to dropping her and Miss Exeter at the public beach. At that moment Antonia, who, just as her mother had suggested, had been crabbing since dawn, appeared on the lawn, streaked with seaweed and exuding a faintly ancient and fishy smell. Dolly was like steel and would not allow her a moment for changing; and so, dropping her crabs and nets on the piazza, Antonia with Miss Exeter got into the car after Dolly, and were duly dropped at the little group of dark-red bathing houses that formed the entrance to the public beach.

Pearl found the child, in spite of her personal untidiness, a most agreeable companion. She had read widely and with imagination. She knew a great deal of poetry—rather martial poetry—by heart; all of Horatius, for instance, which she said she usually recited to herself in the dentist's chair and from which she gained comfort.

They were walking up the wide steps to the bathing house as she spoke, and she stopped and bent down to examine a boy's bicycle—she was a connoisseur of bicycles.

They came in sight of the beach now—all set out with bright-colored umbrellas like gay poisonous mushrooms. It was the hour when the beach was given over to children.

Pearl was thinking that it looked very pretty, when once again she heard Antonia's clarion voice break out at her elbow.

"Hi, there, you kids! Leave that fort alone! It's mine!"

She darted down the narrow boardwalk toward an immense hole in the sand, scattering a band of neatly dressed children, much as the effete Romans were scattered by the first onslaught of the northern barbarians. Pearl could not help laughing as she saw children run to their governesses or snatched back by their nurses; but the next moment she was sorry, for she saw that it was being said in various tongues that Antonia was quite the worst brought-up child in the world. Pearl was nothing if not a partisan, and she was already completely on Antonia's side.

She and Antonia were supposed to bathe early so as to leave the two Conway bathhouses free for Mrs. Conway and Dolly when they appeared at a later and more fashionable hour. "Everything in our family is done for

Dolly," said Antonia when she was finally dragged out of the water. "It makes me tired the way mother indulges every whim of hers."

Rebellious or not, however, Antonia was dressed—as much dressed as she ever was, which was about three-quarters as much as other little girls—by half after twelve.

She and Pearl went back to the beach and sat down under the red-and-black-striped umbrella which the life-saving man had stuck in the sand for them as if he were about to do a pole vault with it. And presently Durland, ready for his swim, came and plopped down beside them, and immediately a girl in a one-piece tomato-colored bathing dress rose from another part of the beach and came and sat on the other side of him.

Antonia, with a thin brown arm, still smelling very slightly of crabs in spite of her swim, clasped about Pearl's neck, blew in her governess' ear the information that this was Caroline Temple, Durland's best girl. Like so many courtships, this one, to the outside world, seemed to be carried on principally by the lady. She neither looked at nor spoke to Pearl and Antonia.

To Durland she said, "Shall we go in now?"

Durland was digging a small hole near Miss Exeter's hand; his shoulder was turned to Caroline and he did not shift it as he replied, "You can if you like."

There was a pause. Apparently she didn't like, for she did not move, and after a time she said in the same tone of lowered confidence, "I have the car here. I'll drive you home."

"Thanks," said Durland. "I'm on my bicycle." Another pause.

"Shall we play tennis this afternoon?"

"I may," answered Durland.

Pearl began to feel her sex pride wounded. She bent forward, and beaming upon the newcomer, she said, "You play tennis?"

Caroline just glanced at her.

"Of course I do," she said.

She had not the smallest intention of being rude, for she was a sweet-tempered child; even less did it occur to her to be jealous of an elderly woman of twenty-four; but her mind, concentrated upon the pursuit of Durland, was rendered irritable by inconsequential interruptions. Durland, however, though no critic of manners, was aware that a gesture of friendship from a goddess had not been gratefully received.

"You might be civil about it," he said, and then looking up at Pearl, he asked in a softened tone of adoration whether she would like to play tennis that afternoon.

"Doubles?" said Caroline, as if this were, of course, possible though utterly undesirable.

"Would you like to play doubles?" Durland asked again.

"If it is convenient to your mother," said Pearl.

Durland dismissed such an idea as repellent to him and, glancing over his shoulder to Caroline, he said, "All right. Miss Exeter and I will play you—if you can get a fourth."

It was not the way Caroline had designed the set and she said so. She said clearly and rather complainingly that she had expected to play with Durland, and yet she did not seem wounded so much as thwarted.

"I'm sure I don't know whom I can get," she said.

"I suppose you can get the faithful Wally—anyone can get Wally."

"I thought you did not like Wally."

"I?" said Durland, as if it were far beneath him ever to have been aware of Wally's existence; and without any further answer he got up and walked into the Atlantic so suddenly that Miss Temple, scrambling as rapidly as possible to her feet, was several yards behind him as he dived into his first wave.

"Isn't she pretty?" said Antonia. "She's been his best girl for two summers."

"I don't think he's very nice to her," said Pearl.

"Well," said Antonia, giving one of her little shakes of the head, "it would seem wonderful to me if Durlie spoke to me at all. However, it may be over. Like what Shakespeare says—one foot on land. Next time I have a chance I'll look and see if her picture is still in the back of his watch."

Presently they were back in the same order—Durland first, and Miss Temple following. He sat dripping, and taking a cigarette from a package he had left on the sand, he began groping for a match.

"Oh, Durland," said Miss Temple, "I do wish you wouldn't smoke. It isn't good for you. It looks so badly." Durland gave a short laugh that seemed to say that if he had regarded public opinion he would have made of life a very different thing. In her distress Caroline turned to the stranger whose presence she had so far refused to acknowledge. "Don't you think it's wrong for him to smoke?" she said.

It was Pearl's moment.

"Why, no," she answered, "I can't see anything wrong about it."

She put out a lazy hand and took one from the little paper envelope. Durland's hand, with the match in it, was arrested.

"But—you're not going to smoke—here? On the public beach?"

"Isn't it allowed?" asked Pearl, all innocence. "It must be—you are smoking. Let me have a match."

"I haven't a match," he said, and threw away his own cigarette so that she could not get a light from that. It was an important moment in his life. He thought rapidly. "I hope you won't think me fresh or anything," he said, "but I don't think a governess ought to smoke, if you know what I mean—not in public anyhow."

She wasn't angry, only thoughtful.

"Well, that's only your opinion."

It touched him that she knew so little of the world—or of her own position. He said gently, "I'm afraid you'd find it was everybody's opinion."

"Ought you to be so much influenced by the opinion of other people?"

"Yes, indeed," he answered. The cigarette with which she was still playing might separate them forever. His mother, he knew, was just waiting for a good excuse to send her away, and where could she find a better one?

She argued it further, tapping the cigarette on her hand as if she were about to place it between her lips.

"But you don't pay any attention when people say you oughtn't to smoke."

Even then he did not know that a trap had been set for him. On the contrary, he thought he had an original idea of some beauty when he said impulsively, "I tell you what, I'll swear off if you will."

She seemed to debate it through an agonizing second or two, while he looked at her with dog-like eyes. Then she smiled and gave him a strong hand.

"All right," she said. "That's a bargain."

Durland felt flooded with joy—not only at having saved a beloved woman but at having done it in just the right way. He picked up the package of cigarettes and flung it toward the sea. It did not quite reach the water and Caroline sprang up and brought it back to him.

"I suppose you thought that was empty," she said.

He tossed it away again without thanking her, but at last to her repeated clamors he yielded the information that he had given up smoking.

"Oh, Durland," she said, "now you can come to the house again. Is that why you did it?"

He did not want to deceive the girl, but he could not resist the temptation of allowing her to deceive herself. He did not answer directly; but rising, he said, "Anyone who wishes to swim to the barrels with me may now do so."

It was more like an invitation than anything he had said all morning, and they were soon swimming side by side.

Presently Mrs. Conway in a dark-blue silk bathing dress with ruffles appeared and dropped a string of pearls into the lap of the governess as if they had been beads. Pearl had never had such pearls in her hands before. They were heavier—much heavier than she had imagined, and brighter, more iridescent, better worth looking at. She was not given to envy, but she was aware of thinking that there was something slightly wrong with a world where Mrs. Conway had pearls and she had not. Antonia insisted on her putting them around her neck.

"It's much safer—you can't drop them in the sand—Cousin Cora always does—that's Miss Wellington; she's no relation, but she likes us to call her cousin—she wants us to call her aunt, but mother says, 'Wait till she is.'"

"Oh," said Pearl, conscious of a distinct pang, "is she going to be?"

Antonia gave one of her head shakes.

"Mother says, 'Say not the struggle nought availeth.' Older people make a lot of fun of their best friends, don't they?"

"Would you like her for an aunt?" said Pearl.

"Yes and no," Antonia replied. "I think the wedding would be fun, and I think I'd be a bridesmaid or something; but as a family we prefer to keep Uncle Anthony to ourselves. Mother says if he marries Cora we wouldn't lose him as much as if he married a stranger. There was a Russian actress one year, with red hair; I didn't think her a bit pretty. She used to send mother flowers and seats for her plays. They were all pretty sad though. Then there was another time—she was married this time, but mother said——"

Antonia broke off to call Pearl's attention to Dolly, who was coming down the boardwalk in a bathing dress of as many hues as Joseph's coat. Everything about her was bent—her back, her knees, her elbows, her fingers, and every crook was obviously intended to charm the young man by whose side she was walking, who was staring out to sea and very thoughtfully putting cotton in his ears. Even Pearl, indifferent as she then supposed herself to be to all men, could not but admit that he was as splendid an example of young blond manhood as she had ever seen. Then as he came nearer she saw a certain pale red-rimmedness about the eyes, and she thought, "He's the kind you'd have to describe as handsome, and yet if anyone else did, you'd say, 'Oh, do you think him handsome? I don't like his looks at all.'"

Antonia meantime was pouring his life history into her ear.

"Allen Williams. He's twenty-one and has been a freshman for two years—isn't he handsome?—and very vicious—gambles and drinks and everything. I heard the Williams' governess telling someone the other day that Monsieur Allen was *déjà très connu dans le monde—le monde gal—gal—*something or other. I wish I knew more French. You can't really tell much what goes on on the beach unless you know French. Of course, he's just amusing himself with Dolly."

"I tell you what I think," said Pearl, suddenly becoming aware that she had been staring, and not only this, but also stared at. "I think it's horrid of you to be against your own sister."

"But look at the way she's giggling and wriggling. I feel ashamed of her," said Antonia.

"That's the very time you ought to stick up for her," said Pearl.

"Well, it's a point of view," said Antonia. "That's what Uncle Anthony always says when he doesn't agree with you but is too lazy to argue it out."

Dolly and Mr. Williams had reached them by this time. Dolly was for passing by, but Williams stopped and said in a voice clearly audible, "And who is the beautiful girl in the pearls?"

Dolly's voice was too low to be audible. She stopped. Spoiled and selfish she might be, but she was at heart a lady. She introduced Mr. Williams to Miss Exeter with perfect civility. Williams took Pearl's hand and looked at her with something fierce and blank in his eyes.

Oh, how well she knew that look!

CHAPTER THREE

That evening Pearl had the satisfaction of writing Mr. Wood that Durland had stopped smoking. She gave the whole scene on the beach. Never before in all her life had she been amused at writing a letter; she had looked upon them as a duty to be paid to friendship. But to this man whom she had never seen she enjoyed writing. It was like patting Alfred—you could express your friendly emotion without fear of rousing any response whatsoever. Almost every day she had some progress to report—Mrs. Conway had consented to keep her jewelry in the safe in her bedroom provided for the purpose. At first she had positively refused, asserting that as she could never remember the combination her jewels remained locked up until an expert was sent down from town to open the safe; and that for her part she would as lief a thief had them, who might get some fun out of them, as that they stayed locked up in her safe for the rest of time. But Pearl very competently offered to make the combination and remember it, and come every morning and get them out at any hour Mrs. Conway chose. A rumor of burglaries in the neighborhood induced Edna to yield.

Then before a week was over algebra became to Durland an illumined subject, a study of mystic beauty and romantic association. He not only mastered it in the proud determination to prove that men were not fools but he invented clever discussions to lengthen his brief hour into an hour and a half; while Antonia, wondering at his industry, kept insisting that it was time to go to the public beach.

All this Pearl wrote, day by day. But she could not write the thing which of all others she knew Mr. Wood wanted to hear—that Antonia was dressed like a nice little girl. The best she could say was that the child was not actually dirty. Nor could she say that she had gained Mrs. Conway's friendship. That lady remained aloof, a little malicious, always in the opposition, treating Pearl's triumphs as petty tyrannies over the children's free spirits, treating Pearl's failures as splendid triumphs in the field of human freedom.

When Pearl appealed to her with "I don't think Antonia ought to wear that torn dress to Olive's for tea, Mrs. Conway," Edna would smile and answer, "You know, Miss Exeter, I can't think those things a matter of life and death the way you do. I own I should be sorry if at eleven she thought of nothing but dress."

"Like Dolly," said Antonia.

That, Pearl discovered, was the secret of Antonia's dislike of neatness. She was afraid of being like Dolly—Dolly, who represented simply everything of which Antonia disapproved.

All this Pearl wrote to Anthony; long, long letters composed after the rest of the household were in bed. "It is long after midnight, and I should be in bed instead of writing——"

She paused. The well-known illustrator who had done her picture for the cleaning-fluid firm had told her—and the illustrator was herself a beautiful woman, experienced in the ways of the world—that all love letters from unmarried girls ended with the words, "But it is after midnight, and I ought to be in bed instead," whether they were written at noon or at night.

Love letters! How absurd!

Letters which amuse the writer to write rarely fail to amuse the recipient to read. Pearl's letters, arriving as they did in bunches, amused him not only on account of their dashing style but on account of the contrast between this style and the pale demure little person he remembered. Anything written day by day gains a serial interest; and Anthony, without newspapers, waited for Pearl's letters as the great interest of life. He had never felt so intimate with his family as through her careful description of them. His sister, though a fairly regular correspondent, had to perfection the art of covering the paper with sentences which by the time they reached her correspondent meant nothing. "I did so wonder whether the preserved ginger I ordered for you had caught your steamer of if the man had mistaken the line—he seemed so stupid——" Pages like this, when he wanted to hear of the contemporary life of the children.

Yet this time the first sentence of his sister's letter interested him:

> She arrived the day before yesterday—your priceless pearl—Antonia's idea of Helen of Troy. But do you think Helen would have made a comfortable sort of governess? This young woman is entirely untrained—turns handsprings on the beach and goes shouting about the tennis courts in a loud Western voice that I do hope the children won't learn to copy. Dolly, who is, as you know, the most sensitively refined being that was ever made, is quite shocked by her. The two younger ones like her well enough, but I can't imagine her ever having any control over them. I always think one must be a little disciplined oneself in order to exercise control over others. I must confess, Anthony, that I should pack your selection off

tomorrow if I had not given you my word to keep her. Cora quite agrees with me that Miss Exeter would do better on the variety stage than as a governess. I don't think there is any news. Durland has entirely given up smoking, as I always said he would—entirely of his own accord. You don't believe me, but a mother has a sort of psychic understanding of her children.

How could he help being on the other side? Yet the letter gave him something to think about. Helen of Troy—that pale, thin girl! Well, he should never understand women's estimates of other women's looks. He laughed aloud over the note about Durland's smoking, Edna and her psychic understanding!

But thinking of psychic things—and far away in the folds of that bare Mexican valley Anthony had time to think—something psychic came from Miss Exeter's letters which he had not felt in her personality. He could not call it exactly conceit, but it was like a conviction of beauty. He did not know how to describe it, but it made him think of an essay by a novelist which he had read, when or where he could not remember—was it by Stevenson?—in which the writer had spoken of the uncontrollable way in which heroines whom you constantly described as lovely kept turning plain and uninteresting on your hands; and the other way round—how heroines, with just a few words of friendly description, suddenly walked through your pages as tremendous beauties, with no assistance from you. Clara Middleton, in the Egoist, had been cited as one of the latter class. Well, it seemed to him that this girl was like that. He had seen her—a nice-looking young woman, but her letters were the letters of a beauty. Probably it was the profound subconscious egotism of the woman coming out. The point was that she was getting away with it. He wrote and asked Durland to send him a photograph of her. But it did not need much diplomacy on the part of Pearl to prevent its ever being dispatched.

As a matter of fact, she did not dread discovery very much. It seemed to her it would be nothing more than an awkward moment—after all, he already knew her better than he had ever known Augusta—only before he came back she must have worked all the desired miracles. Far from dreading his return, she looked forward to it with veiled excitement—great fun, like taking off your masks at a fancy ball.

She had been with the Conway family almost a month when she witnessed the first trial of strength between the hostile factions—Dolly against Antonia. There was only one spare room in the cottage since the governess had come. Dolly announced at luncheon, very casually, that she had invited Allen Williams to spend the following Sunday with them. Antonia broke out at once with the passionate sense of defeat that betrays the young. She had invited her best, indeed her only, friend Olive, who was to be abandoned by her family, for the coming Sunday.

"You said I could ask her, mother. I did ask her—you let me ask her. I asked her first—before Dolly asked Allen—you said I could"—over and over again; but Dolly's flashing silence was more impressive. Pearl knew that it was not so much a question of justice as of trial by torture. Mrs. Conway would yield to whichever of her children could inflict the most pain upon her, and that, of course, was Dolly. Dolly did not reiterate her position like Antonia. Now and then she dropped a frigid sentence that revealed her argument. Her mother had always told her she might ask anyone she liked for week ends. She had asked Allen and he had accepted. As for Olive, she lived in Southampton—why shouldn't she stay in her own house? It was just as an excuse for little girls to sit up talking all night and steal food out of the pantry and get the whole household upset.

This was shrewd. The last time Olive had come to stay it had resulted in the loss of a cook. Mrs. Conway remembered this as Dolly spoke. Her position was painful. She had promised Antonia she could have her friend this Sunday, when Olive's parents were away. But then on the other hand she had also encouraged Dolly to ask anyone she liked to the house. Yet she disliked young Williams and feared Dolly's growing devotion to him. Somebody had already said to her that it was a pity for Dolly to make herself so conspicuous with him—he was no good, that young man. But part of her tragedy as a mother was that she sympathized with her children when thwarted in something in which she knew they ought to be thwarted. She knew now that Dolly's hold on young William's interest was of the slightest; she knew that the girl had obtained this promise of a week end visit with difficulty—perhaps even it was mere convenience—he wanted to go to some party, or to see some other woman. Mrs. Conway knew that if she decided in favor of Antonia, as perhaps strict justice would demand, there never would be any other week end for Williams. Dolly would lose him; and though this was exactly what she desired, she could not be so cruel as to bring it about. So she decided in favor of her elder daughter, and managed as usual to anger both of them.

"I'm afraid, my dear," she said to Antonia, as if she were being particularly impartial, "that this is one of those terrible occasions on which you are called upon to be unselfish and noble and all that. I own I don't care for this young man who says bur-r-rud and wor-ruld, and seems to me to be quite the dullest person I ever met; but Dolly is older than you, you know, and must be allowed to have her playmates first. When you are a big girl and want to have beautiful young morons to stay——"

"I hope I shan't ride roughshod over other people's rights," said Antonia with snapping eyes.

"I'm sorry my friends must be insulted, mother, just because I have ventured to invite them to your house. Believe me, if I had a house of my own I would not trouble you either with my friends or myself."

Tears rose to Mrs. Conway's eyes. She was so deeply hurt she could not even pretend that she wasn't; so hurt that she spoke naturally to the governess when for a second after luncheon, owing to the withdrawal in opposite directions of her two daughters, she found herself alone with the interloper.

"Young people are so cruel," she said. "What more could I do for Dolly? I sacrifice poor little Antonia, I make the house hers—and she tells me practically she only stays with me because she has to."

As Pearl went upstairs Dolly called her into her room—the first time she had ever done such a thing. But after all the woman with all her faults had the virtue of not being a member of the family.

"You see what I mean, Miss Exeter," she said, looking up from polishing her nails with a feverish rapidity. "Everything in this house is done for Antonia—or would be if I did not fight for my rights. Nobody likes to make a scene, but to ask a man like Mr. Williams—you don't know, but women—older women—married women—like Mrs. Temple—so silly—it just bores Allen; but he feels he ought to go there, and when he said he would come here instead, fancy my having to put him off because Antonia wanted that fat Olive to come, when Olive lives here anyhow."

Pearl's limpid gray eyes gazed at her sympathetically. It was her nature to be sympathetic, and presently Dolly was telling her how she had first met Allen, how he had danced and how wonderfully their steps went together. It seemed as if she had remembered every syllable that had ever fallen from his lips, and loved to repeat them, though they were of a conspicuously commonplace character. Then she confided a secret—he had asked himself. She would never have dared to ask him.

"Dared!" said Pearl, every inch the feminist.

"Oh, well," Dolly retreated rapidly, "this house is so full of uninteresting children like Antonia and Durland—under your feet all day long; but when Allen said himself, telling how he didn't want to go to the Temples, 'Why don't you ask me?'——"

Her voice softened over the remembered tones; of course she had asked him.

Pearl's heart sank at this news. She wondered if she were vain to attach a dread significance to his initiative. She remembered that peculiar fierce stare from those pale eyes. Well, she wouldn't speak to him—that was all there was to that.

Presently she left Dolly and went to knock on Antonia's door, which was suspiciously shut; usually Antonia lived and dressed open to corridors.

Yes, as Pearl feared, Antonia was lying on her bed, crumpled as to clothes and damp about the cheeks. Miss Exeter could see now, she said; she was treated like a step-child. Her mother didn't love her as she loved Dolly, and how could anyone love Dolly?—that's what she couldn't understand.

Pearl had not thought it worth while to try to argue Antonia's case with Dolly, but the child was so clear-minded she did try to put Dolly's side of the case to her. Antonia admitted it all, but impatiently.

"And why is he willing to come," she said—"a man like him? He's just making a convenience of Dolly, or something. He doesn't think anything about her at all."

It was exactly Pearl's own impression. Then why was he coming?

He came on Friday afternoon by the fast train, and Dolly in her new pink hat and her white motoring coat—just back from the cleaner and smelling a little bit of gasoline, but so much more becoming than her gray one—went to meet him. She and Allen and Mrs. Conway were all dining out that evening, and Pearl had organized a picnic for herself and Antonia and Durland, far up the beach, with the moon and a fire of driftwood and a great deal of excellent food. They did not see the house guest that evening.

The next morning at half past nine Pearl was obliged to go to the garage to find Antonia; she was studying the oiling system of the green car. There was nothing unfriendly in her attitude to study; she was perfectly willing to learn, if she could only manage to remember that lesson time had come.

They had lessons on the piazza. Pearl, looking out over the dazzling sea and thinking how pleasant a swim was going to be, had said "How do you spell 'separate,' Antonia?" and Antonia, twining her bare toes about the calf of the other leg, had got as far as "Well, I know it's an *e* where you expect an *a* or just the other way," when Williams, bending his head slightly under the curtains, stepped from the dining room upon the piazza.

He looked extremely polished and soaped. He had on white trousers, a gray coat, a blue tie. Antonia, who had never seen him so near before, stared at him, forgetting even to say good morning. He bowed rather formally to the governess, but to Antonia he said, "Where were you last evening? I was watching for you and you didn't appear."

He sat down and drew her toward him with an immaculate brown hand.

Pearl had never seen Antonia embarrassed before. The child kept glancing up at Williams as if fascinated, and glancing quickly away again as if dazzled. Then she turned both knees inward, seemed to dig her toes into the boards and answered in a low, husky voice that they had been out on a picnic.

"I think you might have asked me," said Williams.

He spoke in that tone of false comedy—as if anything you said to a child must be ridiculous—that was peculiarly annoying to Pearl.

Antonia bent her head and muttered that she had not thought he would have enjoyed it.

"I should have enjoyed it," he said, and drew Antonia closer, so that over her head he could give Pearl a hard, significant look.

Pearl rose to her feet. This was a situation she understood thoroughly. She was not going to lose another job on account of a man—a boy rather, younger than herself. In spite of Williams' protests and teasing efforts to retain the child, she swept her up to her bedroom to finish her lessons. But she no longer had Antonia's full attention.

When asked again to spell "separate," Antonia answered, "He is handsome, isn't he?"

"Not to my mind," Pearl answered firmly. "He's clean and healthy looking."

"He's beautifully clean," said Antonia. "Think of going about with someone like that!" The measure of her collapse might be taken when a few minutes later she dashed to the window to watch him drive away with her sister, and turning back she exclaimed sadly, "Gee, I never thought I'd wish I was Dolly!"

Pearl thought to herself that there was no great difficulty in seeing through this young man's plans. He wasn't the kind who wept on the desk like the third vice president of the Encyclopedia company. No, he was going to use Antonia's open admiration as an avenue to the governess. Well, the situation could not prolong itself. This was Saturday, and he would be going early Monday morning. There oughtn't to be much trouble in keeping out of his way. She could count on Dolly's coöperation. She sighed, wishing that Mrs. Conway were more friendly. Dolly would keep him playing golf as late as possible; they would not meet again until luncheon, and that was perfectly safe.

She miscalculated. Williams' will was stronger than Dolly's. It was a day of long, regular waves, high but without force, turned back from the shore by a northerly wind. Antonia was standing near shore diving them, wave after wave, and shaking her short hair out of her eyes after each one passed over her head. Pearl had swum out beyond the line of breakers and was sitting on a barrel, enjoying the sensation of being pulled gently in and out as each swell rolled past her. Suddenly on the shore she saw Williams and Dolly appear in their bathing things. She understood it all. Dolly had been lured to the beach at this early hour by the idea of an undisturbed tête-à-tête. The girl sat down, as if confident that Williams was going to do the same, but he stood gazing out to sea. Pearl felt his eyes reach her, and then he dived into one of the great crested billows and she saw that he was making straight for her barrel. He was coming fast, but he was coming under water. When he reached the barrel Pearl was not there. Looking back, he saw her almost at the shore.

He was, however, the kind of man in whom opposition rouses a sort of malignant persistence. All through luncheon she kept catching his pale eye. She thought Durland noticed it, and hoped that Dolly didn't. Antonia hardly moved her eyes from his face.

After lunch, when they were all in the sitting room, Antonia ran away to get him a match before anyone else had noticed he needed one. Dolly smiled.

"What's this, Allen?" she said. "Is Antonia another of your victims?"

Williams frowned, not because he was in the least annoyed but to indicate that he was a man impervious to flattery. Pearl had one of her inspirations.

"If it's true," she said, "Mr. Williams has it in his power to do us all a great favor. Do ask him, Dolly, to say to Antonia that he likes to see a little girl neatly dressed like other little girls."

"That would, indeed, be a miracle," said Dolly, not wanting anything Allen might accomplish to be underestimated.

"Certainly, if I can," said Allen, looking at the governess.

Pearl was standing turning over the papers on the table, ready for flight, although with Durland and Dolly both in the room she felt perfectly secure. She was delighted with her idea.

"It would be a great help in my life," she said, "if you would." And she looked straight at him and smiled as if she saw before her a combination of a god and a saint. It was a look that went straight to his rather stupid head, through which all sorts of ideas began to dance brightly.

"And what do I get out of it?" he asked.

Dolly laughed. "Oh, Allen," she said, "you must not be so mercenary."

And Pearl, avoiding his hard, demanding eyes, slipped quietly out of the room just as Antonia returned with the matches.

Pearl had not been in her room more than five minutes when a knock came at the door, instantly followed by the entrance of Antonia. The first impression was that the child was in physical pain. Her whole face was trembling, her hand was clasped over her mouth, and the instant the door was shut behind her she burst out crying.

Mr. Williams had said she was dirty!

Pearl, full of pity and feeling horribly guilty, denouncing Williams in her heart as a heavy-handed idiot, could not but marvel over the power of romantic love. Everyone, even the adored Durland, had been saying for years that Antonia was dirty, and eliciting nothing from her but pitying smiles; and now this agony of shame and remorse was occasioned by the same words from a total stranger.

Suffering like this, Pearl knew, could be allayed only by action. She invented action. Antonia should appear for church the next morning, clean, faultless, perfect in every detail. Antonia shook her head dumbly—she had nothing—it was Saturday and all her white dresses were in the wash—her light-blue crêpe de chine had raspberry-ice stains on it—and she had hidden it away; her green linen was covered with motor oil. Mrs. Conway's maid had long ago refused to take any responsibility for Antonia's wardrobe, and Pearl could not blame her.

But the value of the plan was its difficulty. Antonia's agony would not have been soothed by anything easy, and this was not easy. It took all afternoon and most of the evening. Under some crab nets a pair of gray suède slippers were found, which Pearl cleaned with gasoline and a little powder; stuffed into the crown of a riding hat to make it smaller was a pair of fine gray silk stockings; her best black hat, worn only once, had fallen into the water and was a ruin; but retrimmed with a pink rose from an evening dress of Pearl's, it looked better than before. At last a crumpled pink linen dress was discovered wrapped about some precious phonograph records. Pearl borrowed the maid's electric iron and went to work at this. She was so tired when she had finished that she omitted, for the first time, her daily letter to Anthony.

Dressing Antonia the next morning was an excitement. The child's spirits had revived so that she could look at the situation with her customary detachment.

"I'm like that thing in the Bible," she said. "I've put away childish things."

"It will be great fun, you'll find, being as nice-looking as you can be," said Pearl.

Antonia nodded.

"But the other was fun too," she said.

Everything turned out exactly as Pearl had intended. Dolly did not come down to breakfast, and Williams did. So, by a miracle, did Mrs. Conway. Antonia's entrance created a sensation—her carefully curled hair, her spotless linen, her long slim legs in their gray silk stockings. Not only Williams but even Durland administered honeyed words of praise. Mrs. Conway approved of her child, but allowed no credit to Miss Exeter.

"It's so silly to worry about those things," she said. "I always knew that she would eventually begin to take care of her appearance. I shall write Anthony that feminine vanity has asserted itself just as I knew it would."

Mrs. Conway and Pearl and Durland and Antonia went to church, accompanied, as Pearl knew they would be accompanied, by Williams. He said it was entirely on account of Antonia—was a privilege to go to church with a little girl who looked as pretty as she did. Although he spoke in an irritating tone, as if you could make fun of a child without a child suspecting it, Pearl saw that Antonia was flattered at receiving any of his priceless attention.

In the few weeks of Pearl's stay she had become attached to the little wooden church on the dunes. She always sat so that she could look out through the door of the south transept, the upper half of which was usually open, and see the ocean; when it was rough it seemed to roll out a deeper accompaniment than the organ's to:

Oh, hear us when we cry to Thee,

> *For those in peril on the sea.*

There was a tradition that this was always sung.

Sometimes an impatient dog would stand on its hind legs and look in, seeking a praying master; and once a wolfhound had bounded over the half door of one transept and, not finding his owner, had bounded out at the other.

During the sermon Pearl, it must be confessed, was engaged in composing her daily report to Anthony. At last she had accomplished the great achievement—at last she could tell him the thing he most wanted to hear. She made up her mind that she would begin: "All through church I looked at Antonia's pretty little profile under a black hat trimmed with pink roses———" Life presented itself to her in the form of her letters to Wood, thus offsetting the sense of loneliness that Mrs. Conway's mocking aloofness caused her. She was still composing when, after church was over, they walked—Mrs. Conway and Williams ahead and Pearl with Durland on one side and Antonia on the other—the few yards that separated the church from the public beach. Antonia's appearance was much noticed.

Pearl heard an elderly gentleman murmur to Mrs. Conway, "Your little daughter is lovely—lovely. Is beauty contagious?" And he gave a glance at Pearl, who was looking perfectly unconscious but caught Mrs. Conway's bitter reply: "Thank you; I see you feel she was never exposed to it before."

For the first time in her life Antonia was the center of a group of boys—many of them in their first long trousers; all with stiff turned-down collars, white against the sunburn and freckles of their summer complexions. They were telling her, with the perfect candor of youth, that she might have been the recipient of their attentions long before this if she had been dressed as she was dressed today.

"How could I go round the links with a girl without shoes?" one conservative had wailed, revealing a hidden struggle. And Bill Temple, Caroline's elder brother, a year older than Durland, and likely to be junior tennis champion, had said loudly in passing, "Gee, the kid certainly looks great in that get-up!" If he had composed "Helen, thy beauty is to me———" all in her honor he could not have given her a fuller joy.

Pearl was so happy that she allowed her generous nature to lead her into making an acknowledgment to Williams. She had just heard him agree to motor to New York after dinner that evening—his stay was a question of only a few hours now, and on the crowded beach———

She looked up at him and said, waves of gratitude and friendliness rolling toward him like a perfume, "We owe all this to you."

He answered without the least change of expression and in a tone that did not carry an inch beyond Pearl's left ear, "Have you any idea what you do to men?—drive them mad———"

She did not answer at all, but stepped back and allowed other people to come between them; and presently, knowing that the Conway car would be crowded, she invited the willing Durland to walk home with her along the beach.

There were a good many outsiders at luncheon, and though Williams followed her closely into the dining room she slipped into a chair between the two children, and all through the meal was aware of Williams' steady, rather sulky stare from across the table.

After luncheon was over she disappeared. She had the afternoon to herself, for Antonia was going out with her mother. Pearl took a parasol and went and sat on the beach, concealed by the jutting of a dune. She took a book with her, but hardly read. She sat there for an hour, and about four, knowing that Dolly and Williams had arranged to play golf and that she would now have the house to herself, she went back, thinking about the Sunday papers. Almost the only hardship she felt in her position was that her rights to the newspapers were not properly respected—the butler, who was a baseball enthusiast, regularly removing the papers to the pantry as soon as Mrs. Conway had read the headlines.

The sitting room was deserted and the newspapers strewn about the table—a condition which should have suggested to Pearl that the room had been too recently occupied for the servants to have had time to come in and put it to rights. But she didn't think of that. She took up the first sheet that came to hand and saw a long illustrated article about the turquoise mines of Mexico, into which she plunged with a thrill of interest. She was standing with both arms outstretched, her gold-colored head a little bent.

Suddenly she felt two hard, masculine arms go round her, a kiss on the back of her neck, another on her reluctantly turned cheek. It happened in a second. As she struggled ungracefully, angrily, she saw over Williams' shoulder the figure of Durland rising from the hammock on the piazza.

If Wood had received that batch of Sunday letters at the mine he would have torn open Pearl's first—as likely to promise the most amusement. But he got them at his hotel in Mexico City, and conscious of great leisure—for he was staying there a week or so on his way home while he dickered over taxes with a governmental department—he adopted a different method. He ranged them before him inversely in the order of interest. They came—first Durland's. He wondered what Durland wanted, for his nephew was never moved to the momentous effort of writing except under the stress of great financial necessity; second, Edna's; third, that of Miss Wellington, who did not write often; and last Pearl's thick typewritten budget.

> *Dear Uncle Anthony*: I know mother is writing her point of view about this, and I want you to know the truth. I was there and mother was not. Miss Exeter could not have helped what happened. If it was any of our faults it was Dolly's—not only for having that kind of a thug to stay but for being as usual an hour late in getting off, so that Miss Exeter thought they had gone. You can imagine how I felt in seeing a great beast like Williams coming up behind her and grabbing her like that. I let him know what

I thought, but I would like to have pasted him one on the jaw. I wish you had been here. Mother is all wrong—a dreadful injustice is being done a very wonderful woman. She is patient, but I don't suppose she will stand much more. I wouldn't if I were her.

Your affectionate nephew,
DURLAND CONWAY

Wood tore open his sister's letter. His thought was, "Impossible!"

Dear Anthony: I am sorry, after the trouble you took ["A lot you are," he thought] that your priceless pearl will really have to go. It has been an impossible situation from the first, but I have loyally tried to carry it through for your sake—you seemed to care so much about it. I have never liked the girl. She has a sort of breezy aggressiveness that I can't stand, and Cora Wellington felt just the same. I did not write you, but that first evening Cora said to me, "Where is Anthony's judgment—sending you a girl like that?" I do not like the effect she has had on the children—taking all the spirit out of poor Durland, and Antonia appeared dressed for church this morning like a little French doll.

However, when Durland discovered her this afternoon clasped in the arms of a detestable young man by the name of Williams—Allen Williams, whom Dolly, poor child, has had spending Sunday, much against my inclination—I did feel that things had reached a point when even you would hardly blame me for getting rid of her. I sent for the girl and told her she must go. I was surprised and, I own, hurt, Anthony, when she answered that you had extracted a secret promise from her not to go until you released her.

I hope you see what a disagreeable and humiliating position you have put me in. I think I should have ignored both her promise and my own, except that the girl has acquired such a hold over Durland and Antonia that they go on like little maniacs about the injustice I am doing her. Dolly and Cora entirely agree with me. However, I have consented to keep her until I get a telegram from you releasing us both. I do hope you will immediately send it on the receipt of this letter.

Wood laid the letter down with a feeling of the most intense surprise. Allen Williams—a young man unfavorably known to him as an admirer of the most conspicuous of the year's Broadway beauties—that man spontaneously interested in a girl like Miss Exeter—a ruthless, stupid young animal like Williams attracted by that pale, honest, intellectual, badly dressed girl—without an effort on her part. No, that was too much to ask him to believe.

He opened Cora's letter. Cora wrote a large, sprawling hand, and her only rule was never to write upon the next consecutive page, so that her correspondent went hopelessly turning her letters round and about to find the end of a sentence. Wood caught "——getting herself kissed in poor Edna's blameless sitting room in broad daylight, and thus getting rid of her and an undesirable suitor of Dolly's at one fell——"

He twisted the letter about, trying to find the end of this, but coming only upon a description of moonlight on the ocean, he tossed it aside and opened that of the culprit herself.

> I regret to say, [it began in vein that struck Wood as none too serious] that I have caused a scandal. A young man called Williams tried to kiss me—in fact he did—when I was reading the paper and didn't even know he was in the house. I should have dealt with him; but Durland, who saw it all, was so cunning and manly, and ordered him out of the house. Your sister is naturally annoyed with both of us and won't believe I was not to blame. She keeps quoting something you once said to Dolly under circumstances described as similar—that no man kisses a girl if he knows it's really against her will. If you did say that, Mr. Wood, you're wrong. If a man wants to kiss a girl something in his psychology makes him feel sure she wants him to. But the loathsome creepiness a girl feels at having a man whom she doesn't like touching her is something no man can possibly understand.
>
> Williams has behaved technically correctly and actually horridly—saying sourly enough that it was entirely his fault, that he alone was to blame, but letting everyone see that he feels I led him on—only that, of course, a gentleman's lips are sealed. However, he was instantly shipped back to New York on a slow train that stops at every station.
>
> As soon as he was gone Mrs. Conway and I had rather a scene. She wanted me to go at once. I said I could not go

> without your permission. She finally agreed to let me wait until you had been heard from. I need not say I shall do exactly as you wish. It will not be particularly easy to stay after this, but I will do it if you wish—or go—just as you telegraph.

Whatever Anthony Wood's faults might be, lack of decision was not usually one of them. He folded the letters neatly on his table, took his panama hat from the peg, went to the telegraph office and sent his sister the following message:

> Letters received. Please keep Miss Exeter until my return. Should be back within two weeks.

And then, rapid decisions being at times dangerously like impulses, he sent a second one to Miss Exeter herself, which read:

> Wish to express my complete confidence in you.

The days before those two messages came were trying ones in the Conway household, which was now divided into two hostile parties—Pearl, Durland and Antonia on one hand; Mrs. Conway and Dolly, occasionally reenforced by Miss Wellington, on the other. Miss Wellington did not make matters any easier by suggesting to Edna that something similar must have taken place in the case of Anthony himself—just what you'd expect from that sort of girl—that hair, that great curved red mouth. She understood from dear little Dolly that Williams had told her—as much as a man could tell such a thing—that he could hardly have done anything else.

What Williams had really said, for few men are as bad as their adoring women represent them, was that her mother was taking the incident too seriously.

Pearl could not have borne life if it had not been for her daily letter, which she continued to write. Mrs. Conway hardly spoke to her; and if she did, she spoke slowly, enunciating every word carefully as if Pearl's moral obliquity had somehow made her idiotic. Durland, loyal to the death, was not much help, because he merely hated his family and scowled through every meal. Antonia, on the other hand, was one of those rare natures who could be an ally without being a partisan.

"Of course," she would say calmly to anyone who would listen to her, "Allen only came here at all in the hope of seeing Miss Exeter, but you can't expect Dolly to understand that."

Anthony's two telegrams arrived one evening at dinnertime and were handed by the butler, one to Mrs. Conway and one to the governess. Pearl's heart sank on seeing there were two. She thought it must mean he was deciding against her; and though she found her present position unpleasant, she did not want Mr. Wood to decide against her. She opened hers and read its few words at one glance. It was not her habit to blush, but she blushed now with a deep emotion—of gratitude and admiration. Not many men would have stood by her, she thought, in a situation like this. She knew where Antonia got her sense of justice. Or, she thought with something very like jealousy, was it really Augusta in whom he was expressing his confidence, not in her at all? Yes, of course, anyone who had once seen Augusta would feel confidence in her.

The next day she settled back to the routine—lessons with Antonia and then with Durland—the public beach—a silent luncheon—then sometimes a little feeble tennis with Antonia; but more often now her mother took the child out with her, as if Pearl were not a proper person to be given charge of a pure young child. Left alone, Pearl would take her book and parasol and retire to the Conway's beach. She seldom read, for, to be candid, she was not a great reader; but she would sit and stare at the empty sea—empty at least if the wind were from the south; but when it turned and blew from the north, then the whole ocean would be dotted with fishing boats out of Gardiner's Bay; and Pearl, lying there idly, would watch the rowboats putting out and taking in the nets. Sometimes Antonia was permitted to be her companion, and then she read aloud to the child. Antonia was in the stage of development when she loved poetry, but poetry of a stirring, narrative quality—The Ballad of East and West, The Revenge, The Burial of Moses. She would lie with her head in Miss Exeter's lap, gazing up into the unquenchable blue of the sky, and say "I'm going to learn that one by heart," and would get as far as the second verse when it was time to go in and dress. After dinner Pearl and Durland would play Russian bank, which he had proudly and lovingly taught her; and Dolly and Mrs. Conway would run over to Miss Wellington's, where they could abuse the governess to their heart's content.

One night—just between night and day—Pearl woke with an overmastering sense of dread. She had been dreaming that the sea, a perpendicular wall miles and miles high, was coming over the dunes. After two or three days of damp heat the waves had been rising; local weather prophets were talking about the August twister. Now, as she sat up in bed, listening and looking into the dark, she became aware that the wind had risen; the wooden house was creaking and trembling like a ship.

She was frightened, as an animal must be frightened without reason and out of all proportion. In the medley of little sounds she thought she detected the sound of something hostile. The pearls—she thought of the pearls.

It would have been easy to lock her door—no, not easy, for as she sat rigid in her bed she found the idea of motion terrifying; but she could have summoned courage to cross the floor and lock the door. Only, Pearl was afflicted by a sense of responsibility.

She turned on her light—that helped her. She was no longer terrified like an animal; she was merely frightened like a human being. She got up, put on her dressing gown and, crossing the hall by a supreme effort of courage, entered Mrs. Conway's darkened room. Perfectly gentle, regular breathing greeted her ear. She knew where the switch was and turned on the light.

Mrs. Conway sat up in bed and said, "Is anything wrong—the children?"

Pearl's fears melted in the face of human companionship. She felt calm again and rather foolish as she explained that she had felt alarmed for no special reason—had thought about the pearls. Mrs. Conway glanced at the closed safe.

"I thought," she said, "that the argument for keeping valuables in the safe was that we could sleep calmly. The safe can't be opened unless you give the combination."

"It was childish of me," said Pearl. "I was frightened."

Mrs. Conway smiled at her more kindly than she had ever done. It was one of the contradictions in her nature that she was physically brave—a fact obscured to most observers on account of her moral cowardice. Like most brave people, she was kind to the timid.

"It's the storm," she said. "It gets on some people's nerves. I hope the roof isn't leaking; it nearly always does in one of these storms. What were you afraid of?"

"I don't exactly know," said Pearl.

"Would you like me to go back to your room with you? Would you like to sleep on my sofa?" Edna asked.

But that was too ignominious. A faint wild dawn was breaking, and Pearl knew that with the night her terror had gone. She went back to bed.

The next morning the wind was still blowing like a hurricane from the south, though the rain had stopped. Great waves were running up the beach, in some places as far as the sand hills, and forming a long, narrow pool at the base of the dunes. As soon as lessons were over Antonia dragged Miss Exeter to the beach—it was no easy matter, for the wind blew the sand stingingly against face and hands. There was no use in going to the public beach that morning, for the bathing apparatus of barrels and life lines had been washed away, the bathhouses were threatened, and there was a rumor that the sea was washing into Lake Agawam.

Pearl and Antonia sat on their own dunes, watching the wild scene, and suddenly Antonia said, "Look here, Miss Exeter, I want to ask you something. Perhaps I oughtn't to."

Pearl had so completely lost any sense of having a guilty secret that she answered tranquilly, "Go ahead."

"Is Uncle Anthony in love with you—like Mr. Williams?"

Ah, Pearl knew what that meant: Antonia had taken a long drive with her mother and Miss Wellington the day before! She picked her words carefully.

"I only saw your uncle once," she said.

"But Allen only saw you once or twice—and look at the darn thing!"

"Mr. Williams is not in the least in love with me."

"Miss Wellington said that some women have the power of rousing———"

"Antonia, I don't want to hear what she said."

"You don't like her, do you?"

"No."

"Shake," said Antonia heartily. "I don't like her, though she's very kind to me; but it doesn't seem to me"—Antonia's voice took on the flavor of meditation—"that she quite tells the truth. For instance, just before Uncle Anthony went away, she telephoned to him one morning and asked him to come over. He was playing a game of parcheesi with me—I'd teased him a good deal to play—and he said he couldn't come, and she—well, I couldn't hear what she was saying, but at last he said, rather ungraciously, 'All right then, I'll come.' And he went, and he took me with him. And we only stayed about ten minutes, although she wanted us to stay longer. And then later at the bathing beach I heard her telling someone that she was late—she was sorry—she couldn't help it, because Anthony Wood came in just as she was starting—of course she adored having him run in like that, but it did take a good deal of one's time—'one's time'—that's what she said. I call that a lie, don't you?"

"I certainly do," said Pearl.

"That's what I like about you, Miss Exeter; you say right out what you think—even to a child." Antonia looked thoughtful. "It's a great mistake not to tell children the truth; it makes it so hard for them to know what to do. For instance, we have an aunt—a great aunt—Aunt Sophia. She's awful, or as you would say, just terrible, but it seems she's going to leave us all her money. Now if mother would tell us that, it would be simple; but she doesn't. She says to be nice to Aunt Sophia because she's such a dear. She isn't a bit a dear. So I had to find out all by myself why mother, who's so awful to most of her relations, is so nice to Aunt Sophia. I did. And it's the same thing about my father. He tried to kidnap me once—at least he met me on my way to school and asked me to take a drive with him. I wouldn't do it. Mother said it was lucky I didn't. But it wasn't luck. It was good judgment. Grown-up people are queer about that. When they do something wise they say it was wise. But when a child does something wise they say it was lucky. Children have more sense than people think; they have to have."

"You have," said Pearl, who had never thought of all this before.

"Now this morning, do you know why mother wanted to get us all out of the house?" Antonia continued.

Pearl felt tempted to say that Mrs. Conway always wanted to get her out of the house, but she merely shook her head, and Antonia went on, "Because she is going to have an interview with my father."

"With your father?" Pearl sprang to her feet. "Are you sure?"

Antonia nodded.

"When mother is going to see father she looks the way I feel as if I looked when I'm going to the dentist—don't you know, you say to yourself, 'I wouldn't think twice about this if I were brave'—and then you think about it all the time. You know, mother doesn't think she tells us everything, but she really does, except about my father. And so, you see, if it's something about my father I always know, because mother's worried without saying why."

This reasoning seemed sound to Pearl. She felt that in order to fulfill Anthony's instructions she must go to Mrs. Conway's assistance at once. She did not like to burst in upon them from the open windows of the sitting-room, and so ran round the house to the front door. A small, shabby automobile was standing in the circle, and as Pearl bounded up the steps a man came out quickly and got into it—a pale man, with long white hands and something of Durland's birdlike quality. She saw that she was too late. She went into the sitting-room.

Mrs. Conway was standing in the middle of the room, supporting one elbow in one hand and two fingers of the other resting against her chin. She looked so white that every grain of rouge seemed to stand out—away from her cheeks. She turned her eyes coldly upon Pearl.

"Well?" she said.

Pearl had not thought at all what she was going to say, and blurted out, "Oh, Mrs. Conway, I thought you might need me! I thought I could help you if—Mr. Wood said——"

Edna, rather to her own surprise, suddenly lost her temper.

"I'm tired of being considered a perfect fool," she said. "Anthony! I know what Anthony thinks—that I'm always going to give Gordon all the children's money. As a matter of fact, I know better than anyone—though it isn't always very easy to say no, no, no, to a man who has been your husband and who insists if he had five dollars he could make a fortune; but I do say it—I always have—always—almost always. It's a little too much to be watched over and lectured by you, Miss Exeter."

After which speech Mrs. Conway left the room.

Luncheon was more than usually silent that day, although Edna attempted to take an interest in the children's morning, asking whether it had been pleasant in the water.

"My goodness, mother," Antonia answered, "have you looked at the water? We'd certainly have been drowned if we'd gone in."

After lunch was over Edna was obliged to address Miss Exeter directly.

"I think you went off this morning without unlocking my safe," she said.

"Oh, I'm sorry," said Pearl.

Mrs. Conway smiled faintly.

"It was quite what I expected—it always happens with safes," she said. "But now perhaps you will get me my pearls."

Pearl went eagerly, and as she went she remembered that she had remembered to unlock the safe—just before she went to the beach with Antonia. Yes, as she thought, the safe was very slightly ajar. She took the long, slim, blue velvet case from its compartment and brought it to Mrs. Conway in the drawing-room.

It was empty!

The surprise was like a physical blow, and yet no one at first supposed that the pearls were actually gone. Mrs. Conway, as so often happens to anyone who has sustained a loss, was instantly severely lectured by her three children on her habitual carelessness.

Then a superficial search was made on her dressing table, on the glass shelves in the bathroom. Then a recapitulation was made—a joint effort on the part of everybody—of just what had occurred since the pearls were last seen.

Everyone agreed that Mrs. Conway had been wearing them at dinner the night before. She had gone to bed rather early, and distinctly remembered that she had put the pearls in their slim blue velvet case and put the case in the safe and shut the safe, which was then automatically locked. She did not remember seeing the safe unlocked in the morning.

No, Pearl explained, the reason for this was that she, Pearl, had knocked at the door about eleven, just after finishing Durland's algebra lesson. There had been no answer, because Mrs. Conway was in her bath—her bathroom opened out of her bedroom. Pearl had been in a hurry, so that she had just run and unlocked the safe and had called to Mrs. Conway that it was unlocked. There had been no one in the room at the time; but the maid—the maid had been Dolly's nurse when she was a baby, and was therefore absolutely above suspicion—had been sewing in the next room.

Mrs. Conway did not contradict this story. She simply raised her eyebrows and said that she had not noticed that the safe was open.

Evidently it must have been open all day long—very unfortunate.

Pearl felt and probably looked horribly guilty. Of course she ought to have looked to see whether the pearls were in their case when she opened the safe. She usually did. She remembered, too, her strange terror of the night before. Was it possible that that had been based on something real? Had she really heard a footstep under the noise of the storm? Could there have been a burglar in the house, hidden perhaps all night, and stepping out at the right moment about noon when the upstairs rooms were deserted?

It was Pearl who insisted on telephoning to New York for a detective. Mrs. Conway at first objected and said she would feel like a goose if the pearls were immediately discovered—caught in the lace of her tea gown, or something like that. But Pearl was quite severe. If there had been a robbery, she knew that every minute was of importance.

Just before dinner she called an agency. Two detectives arrived by motor about ten o'clock that night. They had a long secret conference with Mrs. Conway. Then one went back to New York and the other—the head man, Mr. Albertson—took up his residence in the house.

Pearl went to bed more worried than ever. It didn't seem to her that the detectives had really taken hold of the situation. She herself could think of a dozen things they might have done that night. It did not occur to her that their first action was to look up the past record of everyone in the household.

CHAPTER FOUR

Human nature being as it is, it is probable that the loss of the pearls was nothing to Edna Conway in comparison with the satisfaction of being able to telegraph her brother that his priceless Pearl was suspected of having stolen them. She was a kind-hearted woman and would not normally have wished to put even the most degraded criminal in prison; but there seemed an ironic justice in the fact that a woman sent to reform the manners of her children should turn out to be a thief. She valued her pearls too. They were not only beautiful and becoming but they had a sentimental association. Her husband had given them to her when they were first married, after a tremendous success at Monte Carlo. They had cost a great deal of money in the days when pearls were cheap, and yet, as he had got them from a ruined Polish nobleman, they had not cost their full value. He had said to her as he gave them to her, "There, my dear, if I never give you anything else——" As a matter of fact, he never had given her anything else; in fact, he had often tried to take them away from her when things had first begun to go wrong. But Edna had managed to cling to them, feeling that they would always keep away that wolf which idle well-to-do middle-aged women appear to dread more than any other group in the community.

Edna was not only kind-hearted but she was normally utterly lacking in persistence; she would not have been able to conceal suspicions from anyone over a protracted period. But malice is a powerful motive, and she managed in the days that followed the loss to play her part admirably. The idea that Anthony was already hurrying home to meet the imposter who had slipped into the real Miss Exeter's place gave her a determination she usually lacked.

It was perhaps stupid of Pearl not to guess that her fraud had been detected as soon as the detectives set to work. But Pearl was so much interested in the recovery of the jewels that it never crossed her mind she herself was suspected. She did notice a slight change for the better in Mrs. Conway's manner—a certain sugary sweetness—a willingness to be in the same room with her, especially if the detectives were for any reason busy—a new interest in all her plans.

The thought that occupied her mind was the idea that Wood was on his way home; that at last she and the man she had been writing to every day for weeks were to meet face to face. How could he fail to be pleased with her—she who had made Antonia neat, Durland studious, and had at least suggested to Dolly's egotism that there were other women in the world at least as attractive as she? Pearl thought a great deal about their first meeting; there would be a certain awkwardness about it, especially if it took place in the presence of the family, as it probably would. Still, she could manage it. She would say in a few simple words that she was Augusta Exeter's best friend, and had taken her place. He was sure to be amused and smile that nice smile which Augusta had described. The interview went on and on in her imagination, a different way each time she imagined it; but always agreeable, always exciting, always ending in Mr. Wood expressing his gratitude and admiration.

Yet this man about whom she was thinking so constantly was actually speeding toward her, feeling as bitter about her as it is possible to feel about a person you have never seen. We forgive anything better than being made ridiculous. It was not mere vanity, though, that made Anthony so angry. He knew that much of his power over his sister had been destroyed. Everything that he suggested in the future would be met by Edna's amused "Another priceless pearl, Anthony." Yes, he said to himself as he sat with folded arms and stared out of the train window, he had made a fool of himself. What did he know of the real Miss Exeter? He had no one but himself to blame.

He had been on the point of starting home when he received Edna's second telegram announcing her loss. Everyone, as the author of Cranford has observed, has a pet economy, and Edna's economy was telegrams. She never cabled or telegraphed if she could help it, and then she usually obscured her meaning by compressing it into as few words as possible. When Anthony opened this one and saw its great length and her name at the bottom of it he knew that something was terribly wrong. It said:

> Pearls stolen from safe. Only governess had combination. Detectives discover she is imposter. Real Miss Exeter married and went to Canada two days after you saw her in New York. This woman has no idea she is suspected. Is closely watched and has had no opportunity of disposing of jewels. Pearls thought to be still on place or hidden on beach. Please return immediately. Be careful about telegrams. She might get them first.

As soon as Anthony read that message he felt a conviction that it was all true. Whether or not she had stolen the pearls, he knew she was an imposter, for he realized now that he had known from the beginning that he had been in correspondence with a beautiful woman. He had tried to tell himself that the quality he felt in her letters was the vanity of a plain one, but all along he had known in his heart that in some strange and subtle way beauty had exuded from every line she wrote. He had been made a fool of by a beautiful and criminal woman. Well, he would hurry home and settle that score in short order. He was not a cruel man, he said to himself, but this did not seem a situation that called for mercy.

It was, of course, necessary that someone should meet Anthony on his arrival in New York and acquaint him with all the details. As Edna was unwilling to leave her household, the duty fell to Miss Wellington, who complained a great deal and leaped at the chance.

So when Anthony got off the train in the Pennsylvania Station there was not only his secretary but his old friend, Cora Wellington, waiting to greet him. The secretary remained to see about the bags, while he and Miss Wellington drove to his apartment. The robbery was still a secret—not to be told to the papers—even the secretary did not know of it. As they drove up the long incline to the level of Seventh Avenue Cora said the thing that Anthony wanted to hear and yet would not say even to himself:

"Really, Anthony, I think Edna might have guessed that it was not the governess you had sent. You couldn't have selected such a person—dyed yellow hair and a sort of exuberant, almost coarse good looks that you wouldn't admire in any woman and would not tolerate in a governess, I'm sure."

It was agreeable to hear, but he would not admit it.

"Poor old Edna," he said. "I don't feel exactly in a position to criticize. This woman must be clever."

"Clever!" exclaimed Miss Wellington. "It's uncanny! Instantly she obtained an almost hypnotic influence over Durland and Antonia. Even Dolly was on the point of succumbing—if it had not been that the woman overreached herself in her affair with young Williams. Between ourselves, Anthony, though I haven't said this to Edna, I don't feel at all sure that that affair did not go a great deal further than the kiss."

Anthony frowned in silence. This was almost more than he could bear. He said to himself that it was the idea of Antonia being brought into contact with such a situation that disgusted him.

Cora was kind enough to sit in his drawing-room and wait while he had a bath and dressed. It was a nice room and she thought as she waited how she would rearrange the furniture if ever she should come to live there. There were photographs of the children about—Antonia as a baby, Durland in his first sailor suit, a picture of Edna with the three children grouped about her like English royalties.

She was wearing the pearls.

Then Anthony came out of his room, looking handsome and sleek and brown and very well dressed in blue serge; and they went out and had luncheon together, and then started at once for their drive of a hundred miles in Anthony's car.

She answered all his questions—and one he did not ask. She volunteered: "I must confess, Anthony, when I first saw this girl—saw how unsuitable she was—I felt your wonderful judgment must have been clouded by your having fallen in love with her."

"Recollect, please," he returned, "that even if it had been the girl I saw, I had only seen her once."

"Don't people fall in love at first sight?"

Anthony smiled.

"I don't," he said; and he went on to describe the slow process by which a love which can be depended on to last must necessarily grow.

To Miss Wellington, who had known Anthony for fifteen years, the description was perfectly satisfactory.

They reached Edna's house a little after five. Dolly had gone away the day before to soothe her wounded feelings at a house party in the Adirondacks. Durland was playing golf and Antonia having supper with her friend Olive. Edna alone received the traveler. She did not reproach him; she gave him the greeting of a woman simply crushed by anxiety.

He said, "I'm awfully sorry about this, Edna. You've had a disagreeable time—aside from the pearls, I mean."

She raised her large sullen eyes.

"If only you had not made me promise, Tony—so that I was not free to turn a thief out of my house until she had actually stolen my valuables. A woman has an intuition when she's allowed to follow it."

He had not a word to say in answer. He had an interview with the detective—the head man, Mr. Albertson; the other one was engaged in watching Miss Exeter—the false Miss Exeter, who was sitting, as her custom was of an afternoon, on the beach. It was this habit of sitting for hours alone on the beach that had led to the theory that the pearls were hidden there, waiting the right opportunity to be dug up and dispatched to a confederate.

Mr. Albertson was a tall, gray-haired man of the utmost dignity. His figure would have been improved by a faithful addiction to the daily dozen, and his feet were extraordinarily large. He had a calm, grand manner and was extremely chivalrous in his attitude toward all women—even those he was engaged in sending to jail. He reminded Anthony of the walrus—or was it the carpenter?—who wept so bitterly for the oysters while he sorted out those of the largest size. Mr. Albertson melted with pity for that sweet young creature as he detailed the growing mass of evidence against her: The burglaries in Southampton since her coming; the fact that she had insisted on having the combination of the safe; the fact that Mrs. Conway had locked the pearls in the safe and that only Miss Exeter had gone to the safe afterward; the mysterious appearance of Miss Exeter in Mrs. Conway's room during the night before the robbery, and, of course, her alias. It had been largely a matter of form, Mr. Albertson said—the sending of his men to look up her record. It had been a shock to them all to find that the agency which had originally sent Wood the names of governesses could offer proof that their Miss Exeter had married and gone to Canada. So far they had not been able to get any information as to this woman who had slipped into her place. Some of her things had a P on them. Mr. Albertson mentioned that there was a notorious English thief—Golden Polly or Golden Moll.

"She's called by both names," said Mr. Albertson. "This girl answers her description very good."

Wood nodded. Had he in fact been getting a daily letter all these weeks from Golden Moll? The idea intrigued him not a little.

"I think I'll go and have a talk with her," he said.

"By all means, by all means," said Mr. Albertson. "We've just been waiting for you, you know—just to see how she'll act when confronted with you. She hasn't a notion, you know, that you've left Mexico. But," he went on in his deep rich voice, "I'd speak her fair if I was you. Kindness, Mr. Wood, never does any harm. What are we put in this world for except to help each other—women especially? If I was you I'd say, 'Look, girlie, we want to help you. We have you dead to rights, and you'd better come across. Come across, girlie,' I'd say, 'and make it easy for everyone.'" Mr. Albertson had already recommended this speech to Mrs. Conway without success, and now it seemed to him that Mr. Wood was not really going to make it.

"Ay, yes," Anthony said rather noncommittally.

He turned from Mr. Albertson quietly, as is some people's manner when they are doing something important and, crossing the piazza, stood a moment at the top of the steps.

The sun had just set behind his right shoulder, and to those who love the sea the bare flat scene had at this moment an extraordinary beauty. All round the circle of the horizon there was a grayish lilac color. The sea was blue and gray, the beach was pink, with gray shadows under the dunes—strange blending colors that come with no other light. The storm was over, and the sea, though not smooth, was heaving with a slow, regular swell. The beach, even to the dunes, was strewn still with seaweed and lumber and all the flotsam and jetsam of a high tide.

Immediately in front of Anthony was a large rose-colored parasol, the owner of which had evidently forgotten to put it down, although for an hour now it could have been of not the slightest use. Nothing appeared beneath it but the tip of a white suède slipper.

Anthony stood and looked, a smile hovering at the corners of his mouth. There she was—possibly the Golden Moll of Albertson's suspicions, certainly the writer of interesting letters, the reformer of his niece's manners, the stealer of the pearls.

Then he heard Antonia's voice behind him, calling his name. Ordinarily she would have stolen up behind him and clung round his neck with her feet off the ground; but now she evidently wanted him to get the full effect of her changed appearance, for she stood ten feet off and spoke to him. Oddly enough, she was wearing the very clothes which Pearl had described—the pink linen, the hat with the pink rose, the gray silk stockings and gray suède pumps. Nothing, Anthony thought, could have been more accurate. The child was very beautiful, just as he had hoped—hardly dared to hope—to see her.

She gave him just that second to take her all in, and then sprang at his neck.

"Oh, don't you think I look nice?" she said passionately. "It's all Miss Exeter—your priceless pearl—and she is priceless. Don't you think I look nice? I like her better almost than anyone I ever knew, because she's so straight. Don't you think I look nice?"

"Indeed I do," said her uncle. He managed to free his neck from the yoke of Antonia's arms and held her off and turned her round. "Yes," he said, "you look exactly as I like to see you."

Antonia smiled and then sighed.

"I feel every stitch I have on," she said, "particularly the shoes and stockings." She raised first one leg and then the other and shook it, with a gesture not at all graceful. "I've never worn them except in winter before. But still, it does make a difference in one's popularity—clothes—particularly with boys. Boys are funny, Uncle Anthony."

Nothing interested Anthony more than to discuss the problems of life with his niece, but at the moment his mind was not sufficiently disengaged. He was sorry to interrupt her, but he was obliged to go and have a few words with her governess.

"That's all right," said Antonia. "I'll go too." And she slipped her arm through his and, leaning her head against the point of his shoulder prepared to descend the steps.

But Anthony explained to her that he wished to talk to Miss Exeter by himself. Antonia was disappointed. She had looked forward to being present when her uncle and the governess met again, but she adjusted herself as usual.

"There's Mr. Albertson," she said. "I'll get him to come and sit with me while I have supper, and tell me stories of crime. He says there aren't any people like Sherlock Holmes, and that stories like that make it hard for real detectives. I suppose that's true, and yet it's horrid to face facts sometimes, isn't it, Uncle Anthony? It makes real life seem pretty dull sometimes."

"Real life is not dull, Antonia," said her uncle, "take it from me."

He watched her safely into a conversation with Mr. Albertson, and then, with his hands in his pockets, he sauntered down the steps, across the sand toward that rose-colored parasol.

"Good afternoon, Miss Exeter," he said pleasantly.

It had been kept a profound secret that Anthony was on his way home. The detectives had pointed out to Mrs. Conway that this was important—that if the woman knew she was about to be unmasked she might be goaded into sudden action—perhaps even into destroying the pearls.

Hearing a strange voice calling her by name, Pearl came out of a trance into which the sunset and the sea had thrown her; glancing up from under her parasol, she saw at once that the speaker was Anthony Wood, and that he was exactly as she had imagined him. Seeing this, her heart gave a peculiar leap, and she beamed at him, more freely and wonderfully than she had ever beamed at anyone in the world. The look affected him—it would have affected any man; not just her beauty, for he had seen a good deal of beauty in his day, but this warm, generous honesty combined with beauty was something he had never seen. For a second or two they just looked at each other, Pearl beaming and beaming, and Wood looking at her, his face like a dark mask, but his turquoise eyes piercing her heart.

She spoke first. She said in her queer deep voice, "Oh, I'm so glad you've come, Mr. Wood."

"Are you?" he said.

Of all the sentences with which she might have greeted him—sentences of excuse, of explanation, of appeal—he had never thought of her saying this, and saying it with all the manner of joy and relief.

"Indeed I am," she went on, still on that same note. "Have you seen Antonia?"

"Yes, I have."

"And isn't she——"

"We'll leave that for a moment," he said, for her effrontery began to annoy him, and his tone was curt. But instead of being alarmed or apologetic, she gave a little chuckle.

"Oh, yes, I know," she said; "of course you want an explanation; only I wanted to be sure you'd seen my great achievement first, for it is an achievement, isn't it?"

His eyebrows went up.

"Do you really expect to be praised for anything you may have done," he said, "before you offer some explanation as to why you are here masquerading as Miss Exeter?"

Pearl's face fell. He was really quite cross. It seemed hard to her that the meaningless sort of beam with which she accompanied a casual good morning had been enough to reduce the third vice president to weeping on his desk, while a particularly concentrated beam—a beam designed to say in a ladylike, yet unmistakable manner that the one man of all men was now standing before her—seemed to have no effect whatsoever on said man. She tried it nevertheless.

Anthony, seeing it, suddenly became angry. Did this woman, he thought, who was perhaps a thief and was certainly an impostor, really suppose she was going to charm him, Anthony Wood, by her mere beauty—he who was well known to be indifferent to women? She would learn——

But what she would learn was not formulated, for she now surprised him by jumping to her feet and running like a gazelle toward the sea, crying out something to him which he did not catch. He started, however, in full pursuit—his first thought being that she intended to drown herself; the second that she meant to fling the pearls into the sea—the well-known trick of destroying the evidence in a tight place. She ran on. The sea was up to her knees—up to her waist, fully dressed as she was; she was now swimming. They had the sea entirely to themselves. Even the detectives, trusting to Mr. Wood, had withdrawn for a bite to eat; and at five o'clock all those fortunate people who come to the seaside for the summer are engaged in golfing or playing bridge, and seem to ignore the existence of the Atlantic Ocean.

Anthony had hesitated at the brink of the sea long enough to take off first his shoes, second his watch and third the light coat which he had worn driving the car, so that he was some little distance behind her. Swimming hard and for the most part under water, he did not see for some time the object which had attracted Pearl's attention. Neither suicide nor the pearls were the object of her plunge, but a small white dog which appeared to be drowning. Some children up the beach had been throwing sticks for it, and now at the end of a long afternoon it had got caught in some current and was obviously in trouble, every third or fourth wave washing over its little pointed nose.

Pearl, never doubting that Wood was actuated by the same motives as herself, panted out, "Can we get there in time?"

He came alongside her now.

"You're not going to drown too!" he said.

She shook her wet head. Together they towed the exhausted little creature back. As soon as she could walk Pearl picked it up in her arms and strode ashore.

"Don't you think it was a crime for those children to go away and leave him like that?" Her gray eyes, instead of beaming, glowed angrily.

"Are you so against crime?" said Anthony, trying to smooth the water out of his hair.

She did not even take the trouble to answer but became absorbed in tending the dog. It was a white dog, at least its hair was white; but now, soaked and plastered to its body, the general effect was of a cloudy pink with gray spots. It was the offspring probably of a spotted carriage dog and a poodle. Between it and Pearl a perfect understanding seemed to have been at once established. She knelt beside it, and suddenly looking up at Anthony with one of her spreading smiles, she said, "I'm afraid it's awfully ugly."

"It has personality," he answered. He could not but be aware that Pearl's thin dress was clinging to her almost as closely as the dog's soft coat.

"Let me have your coat," she said.

He held it out, expecting that she meant to put it on, for every line of her figure was visible, and every line was lovely. But Pearl was utterly unconscious of herself. She took the coat and wrapped the dog in it, so that only its head stuck out, with its adoring eyes turned to her. As he watched her he found he knew positively that she had not taken the pearls. It was no logical process; he did not say, "This girl is too kind or too generous or too without selfconsciousness or too much at peace." Perhaps it was a combination of all these ideas, or perhaps it was just the miracle of personality; but somehow or other he knew positively and for all time that she was not a thief; that she, on the contrary, was just what in his opinion a woman ought to be. He looked down at the bent golden head, dripping pure drops of crystal. Dyed! What a spiteful goose Cora Wellington was!

Then Durland came down the steps.

"What's happened?" he asked.

"We've been rescuing a dog," said Anthony. "Miss—Exeter and I." So far he knew no other name for her.

Durland smiled at him above her head, as much as to say, "Could anything be more ridiculously attaching than women are—this woman in particular?" And Anthony smiled back in a similar manner.

Then there was a shout, and Antonia, having finished her supper and exhausted at least for the moment Mr. Albertson's narrative powers, came flying down the steps, eager to know why it was that Miss Exeter and her uncle had been in swimming with their clothes on. When explained, it appeared to her the most natural thing in the world.

"Isn't he sweet?" she said, when she had heard the story. "I think Horatius would be a good name for him—on account of 'Never, I ween, did swimmer, in such an evil case, struggle through such a raging flood'—you know. Do you think mother will let us keep him? Or do you want to keep him, Miss Exeter? Oh, dear, I suppose you do!"

"No, I can't," said Pearl, with regret. "I'd like to, but Alfred hates dogs."

Anthony was surprised to hear his own voice saying sharply, "And who is Alfred?"

"He's my cat," said Pearl, turning her whole face up to him. "Everyone says he's very ugly, but I love him."

They smiled at each other; it was so obvious that Anthony refrained from saying, "Lucky creature."

Presently they moved toward the house—first Pearl, bearing Horatius still wrapped in Anthony's motoring coat; then Durland, most solicitous lest the dog should be too heavy for Miss Exeter; then Anthony carrying his shoes and coat and waistcoat; and then Antonia, dancing about. They approached the house in a quiet and rather sneaky way, by the kitchen entrance. Anthony had no wish to meet his sister, who supposed that he had been grilling a criminal. The children felt grave doubts that their mother would welcome Horatius at all—not that she was a cruel woman, but that she feared strange curs about the house. Fortunately the cook, who had a great weakness for Antonia, was cordial, and allowed Horatius to dry out behind the kitchen stove.

It was now high time to dress for dinner, so there was a good excuse for stealing softly up the back stairs.

While Anthony was tying his tie a knock came at the door, and Edna came in with the manner of a person confidently expecting important intelligence.

She said in a low voice, but with an immense amount of facial gesticulation to take the place of sound, "Albertson told me you had an interview. What did you find out?"

For the first time Anthony realized that he had been an hour in the company of the false Miss Exeter without having even asked her true name. He might at least have done that. A weak man would have answered irritably that what between stray dogs drowning and Edna's children interrupting he had not had an opportunity to ask the woman anything. But he was not weak. He simply told her the truth. He saw that she accepted the story with reservations. A drowning dog was all very well, but how about her pearls?

Dinner ought to have been a terrible meal, with Edna bitter and suspicious and the two detectives looking in at the window every now and then—just to show that they were on the job; but, as a matter of fact, it was extremely gay and pleasant. Antonia was allowed to hover about the room in honor of her uncle's return, and Pearl and Anthony were—or appeared to be—in the highest spirits.

Need it be recorded that Pearl had on her best dress? It was a soft, black, shining crêpe which she had run up one afternoon in the spring when she felt most depressed about not being able to find a position. Dressmaking often lightened her black moments; it was to her an exciting form of creation. It had been quickly and casually done, but it had turned out well. Round her neck she wore the silliest little string of bright blue-glass beads, which someone had once given a doll of Antonia's in the dead past when Antonia played with dolls, and which Antonia herself occasionally wore. Antonia had left them in Pearl's room, for her new-found personal neatness did not as yet extend to the care of her possessions, and in an impulse Pearl had put them on and found the result good. So did Antonia.

"Oh, see!" she said as they sat down at table. "She has on my beads."

"Fancy Miss Exeter wearing someone else's beads!" said Edna in a tone hard to mistake for a friendly one.

"But don't they look well on her?" said Antonia. "Uncle Tony, don't you think they look well on her? How could you describe her as 'of pleasing appearance'? It nearly made me miss her at the station that first day. I went dodging about, trying to find a pale, plain girl—that's what mother told me to look for. I think Miss Exeter is beautiful, don't you?"

"Antonia!" said her mother scornfully, as if nonsense were being talked.

Anthony, however, never allowed his niece to put him in a hole.

"I certainly do," he said, and he looked straight at Pearl, and she looked straight at him and laughed and said, "You'd be a brave man to say no when Antonia takes that tone."

"I should be worse than brave—I should be a liar," said Anthony.

The sentiment, which brought a lovely beam from Pearl, brought him a dark glance from his sister. She thought it was not like Anthony to be silly about a woman, and then the encouraging idea occurred to her that he was luring her on in order to win her confidence—clever creature that he was.

As soon as dinner was over the children rushed away to feed Horatius; and Edna, who felt the need of uninterrupted conversation with her brother, led him across the lawn to Miss Wellington's house. It was not easy, for he showed the same reluctance to go that people show toward leaving a wood fire on a cold day; but when Miss Exeter—who, of course, everyone knew wasn't Miss Exeter—said she had a letter to write he rose to his feet.

"A letter?" he said, the idea being, of course, that now he was at home, there could be no more letters in the world.

Pearl nodded. It really was important, for she had always promised Augusta to write her a full account of the first meeting with her respected employer; and, as a matter of fact, Pearl was bursting with eagerness to express her emotion to someone. If she wrote at once the letter could be posted that evening, when, about nine o'clock, a man came to deliver and receive mail.

As Edna and her brother went out they passed Mr. Albertson on guard, and Edna conveyed the information to him that "she" had gone to write a letter. Albertson made a reassuring gesture and they passed on.

Cora was all eagerness and cordiality.

"And what has Anthony discovered about her?" were her first words—spoken to Edna, but directed toward him.

Edna came nobly to his assistance, gave an account of the rescue of Horatius quite as if she thought it a natural, explainable incident, which she was really very far from thinking.

"And what are his impressions?" said Cora.

Anthony found this question almost as embarrassing as the first one. He could not share his impressions. They were mingled—that the girl was beautiful—that swimming was a sensuous and graceful motion—that wet garments clinging to lovely limbs had not been sculptured since the Greeks made statuettes—that absolute integrity is consistent with masquerading under another name than your own and stealing someone else's references. But, alas, these convictions were as impossible to share as a religious revelation. He turned for help to the most ancient methods.

"And what do you think of her, Cora?" he said, as if he really cared.

"I wrote you what I thought," said Cora, and went into it again, while he sat smoking and trying to remember whether or not he had ever read that letter of Cora's with the long description of moonlight on the sea. He rather thought he hadn't.

"Ah," said Edna, willing to do Cora a kindness, "so you and Anthony correspond, do you?" At which Cora laughed self-consciously, and Anthony looked like a graven image—his well-known method of concealing emotion. This time the emotion was simply irritation, but Edna said to herself, "Well, after all, she wouldn't be so bad."

In the short pause that followed, Durland bounded suddenly into the room. His eyes, which were normally blue like his mother's, looked almost white in the sudden lights of the room. They were very wide open, and his small face was pale under his freckles and set with anger.

"Look here, Uncle Anthony," he said, "did you know what is going on in our house? Did you know they suspected Miss Exeter of stealing mother's pearls?" No one answered, and he continued, his voice shaking a little: "She asked me to give a letter she had been writing to the man who comes with the evening mail, and as I did Albertson came out and tried to take it from me—but that was a little too much." The letter was still in his hand, crumpled from the struggle. "I never heard of such a thing! It's an outrage! Did you know of this, mother?" There was something menacing in his tone.

"My dear boy," said Edna, in that patronizing tone that people use as if their ability to conceal something from a child were a tremendous proof of their own superiority. "I'm afraid it will be a great shock to you, but you must face the fact that she did steal my pearls—at least so we believe; and that she is not Miss Exeter at all—she is a notorious English jewel thief known by the agreeable sobriquet of Golden Moll."

"You don't know that, Edna," said her brother quickly.

"I should say not!" cried Durland. "Mother, I think it's perfectly rotten of you to think it's even possible."

Edna turned to her brother.

"You see, Anthony," she said, "what you've done to me, introducing this woman into my house—turning my own children against me."

Cora smiled at the boy soothingly.

"But Durland doesn't know that we have proof that she took the pearls," she said, as one calmly able to make all smooth and easy.

"No, Durland," said his mother, "I have not been able to tell you—the detectives would not let me until your uncle got back—that we have proof. Miss Exeter is not Miss Exeter at all—just an imposter. Oh, tell him, Anthony—tell him that she's—a common, everyday thief."

"I can't do that," said Wood, "because I don't think so."

"You mean," said his sister, as if now, indeed, a chasm had opened at her very feet, "that you have any doubt that she stole the pearls?"

"I'm perfectly certain that she didn't," said Wood.

Edna burst out at this into a wail of reproach and anger, ending with the not unnatural accusation that her brother must be in love with the woman too.

"Yes, perhaps I am," said Anthony.

The idea was new to him, and not repugnant; but he spoke more to annoy his sister than from any more serious motive; but as he spoke he saw that Pearl and Mr. Albertson were in the room and must have heard him, Pearl, however, was too much excited already to register any further excitement. She strode into the room as she strode into the board room of the Encyclopedia; and almost at once catching sight of her letter, still in Durland's hand, she made a grab for it; only Edna was quicker—or rather nearer—and succeeded in getting it first. Pearl turned to Anthony.

"Mr. Wood," she said, "I want my letter—I won't have anyone read my letter. It's an outrage!"

Mr. Albertson felt his moment had come.

"Now look, girlie," he said, "we about have the goods on you. Think of your folks! We want to help you." He took the letter from Mrs. Conway. "I know," he said, "that a lady's correspondence ought to be sacred, but——"

"But," said Edna, not able to refrain from interrupting—"but ask her why it is she doesn't want her letter read."

"Well, I reckon I can figure that out for myself," said Mr. Albertson.

But in this instance—perhaps the only one of his long and successful career—he was wrong. He could not figure out why it was Pearl objected so violently to allowing that letter to be read.

The reason was this: She had always promised Augusta that she would communicate her first impressions of Mr. Wood, and as soon as he and his sister left the house to go to Miss Wellington's she had run upstairs, and on the much-used typewriter she hastily ticked out a prose lyric on the subject of her meeting with the only man she ever could have or ever had loved. It began:

> My dear, he came this afternoon. Why didn't you tell me what he was like? Oh, I know you said he was attractive. Attractive! He's incredible! He's devastating! And that voice! You never said a word about that voice, which makes me shake every time he speaks—like a telegraph wire in a wind. Oh, Augusta, isn't it silly? But I think I love him——

That was just the way it began.

At the sight of that letter in Mrs. Conway's hands, a storm of emotion swept over Pearl, even before she remembered just what she had said. But as phrase after phrase flashed before her eyes and seemed actually to tingle down to the tips of her fingers, she sprang like an animal at its prey, and would have had it, too, if it had not been for Mr. Albertson, who catching her elbow as she went by, not only stopped her, but spun her completely round—so vigorous had been her motion.

Frustrated in action, Pearl burst into speech. She said that she must and would have that letter back; she said that opening other people's letters was a state's prison offense; she went on like a maniac, and every word she uttered made Mr. Albertson feel more and more convinced that the letter must be read. Still, he was a chivalrous man; he believed in chivalry as some people believe in Christianity—as the important highway in their lives, from which at moments they are obliged to stray.

"Now look, girlie," he said again, in accents even more honeyed, "don't excite yourself. Why would you mind me reading your letter, which I see is to another lady?"

"It's none of your business why I mind," said Pearl. "I just do. Oh, Mr. Wood," she said, turning to Anthony, "don't let them read my letter!"

"I won't," he said. "I'll read it myself."

"Oh, no!" said Pearl with a little scream.

There was a pause. Anthony already had the letter in his hands now. He looked very gravely at Pearl.

"I'm sorry you mind," he said. "But this letter must be read either by my sister or me or Albertson. Which one would you rather have read it?"

It was a hard choice. Pearl looked deliberately from one to another, and then she looked at Anthony.

"You," she said.

In complete silence he opened it and read it carefully through. Pearl stood motionless, watching him, studying his face. If he had laughed, if he had even smiled, she would have killed him. She was hardly aware of Albertson and Edna and Cora and Durland, all also watching him, to read in his face what he was reading on the paper. None of them read anything. His face was like a mask. He folded the letter and replaced it in the envelope. Then he took out his pocketbook and put the letter in it and put the pocketbook back in his pocket.

Then he said, "I wish to have a word with Miss Exeter alone." There was a small room that opened off the room in which they were sitting; he walked toward it. "May we go in here, Cora?" he said. He made a motion with his hand, and Pearl, like a person bewitched, preceded him.

"Don't be long, Tony," Edna called to him.

"I may be some time," he answered, and shut the door behind him.

Five minutes passed—ten. To those waiting it seemed an hour. Once Mr. Albertson walked near the door and bent his head.

"Can you hear anything?" said Edna.

"Not a thing," said Mr. Albertson.

"You wouldn't be such a cad as to listen, would you?" said Durland.

Nobody answered him. More time elapsed; and then Albertson, springing up, walked with a firm step to the door and turned the handle. It was locked. Albertson shook back a long gray lock from his forehead.

"What do you make of that?" he said.

Miss Wellington laughed.

"Mrs. Conway has the right explanation, I think," she said. "She's done the trick with Mr. Wood too."

"Not at all," said Edna. "How can you be so low, Cora? I only said that to make Anthony angry. He's finding out—luring her to tell him everything."

"Kidding her along, you mean?" said Mr. Albertson, who hated people not to use the right word.

"They've probably both got out of the back window by this time," said Miss Wellington.

This time Mr. Albertson frankly leaned his ear against the crack of the door.

"No, they're there yet," he said, moving away again. "I can hear them talking—low."

Another silence succeeded to this information, and then Mrs. Conway's butler appeared in the doorway. He looked about and said over his shoulder, "Yes, sir, she's here." He drew back and ushered in Gordon Conway.

Edna looked at the man who had been her husband and said irritably, "You, Gordon; This is really a little too much!"

"Hullo, father," said Durland.

"Hullo, Durlie," said his father, as if he were trying to be cordial; and then, seeing Albertson, he added in a tone really cordial, "Why, Albertson, how do you do? I haven't seen you since the night what's his name—who had that crooked wheel in Hester Street—was pulled. Off the force?"

The two men shook hands.

"Gordon," said Edna, again determined to know the worst, "what do you want?"

"Why, oddly enough—nothing at all," replied Mr. Conway.

He did not give the same impression of furtiveness and wasted pallor that Pearl had gained when she had caught a glimpse of him on the steps. No one could say he had a color, but he was distinctly less corpselike. There was nothing shabby about him now either. He was very well dressed in a dark morning suit; his boots, his tie, the wrist watch which he kept glancing at as if his time was rather short, were all of the most elegant sort.

"No, my dear," he went on, "you ought to welcome me most cordially, for I have come to make you a present—quite a present." And fishing languidly in his pocket he produced the string of pearls.

"A present!" cried Edna. "Those are my pearls!"

"They are now," said her husband politely, "because I have made up my mind to give them to you."

"You gave them to me originally—they were always mine."

Conway shook his head a number of times.

"So you have always said, Edna; but saying a thing over and over again does not make it any truer. I did not give them to you——"

"You did," said Edna.

"Ah, Edna," he answered sadly, "how you can take the grace out of life! You can make even the present of a splendid string of pearls seem ungracious. I never gave them to you. I let you wear them while you were my wife—a mistake, for when you ceased to be my wife you would not give them back—natural, but hardly honest."

"That's absolutely untrue," said Edna.

He did not allow her to ruffle him.

"But now," he went on, "I do give them to you—freely and completely. Be witness, Albertson, that I present this string of pearls to this lady—who was once my wife."

Edna was examining them pearl by pearl.

"They seem to be all right," she said. "The number is right. What's this?" she added, indicating an emerald drop which had never been on them before.

"That's an extra; that's interest on the money," answered Conway with a flourish; "that's an expression of thanks for your courtesy in letting me have them at a moment when they meant so much to me."

This recalled the question of how he had obtained them. "Gordon," she said, "did you steal those out of my safe?"

He shook his head. "You can't steal what is already your own."

"I can't see how in the world you got them," said Edna, "unless that woman is a confederate. Did she give them to you?"

"I don't even know what woman you mean, Edna," he answered. "If you mean a magnificent Hebe who was coming into the house in a hurry as I was going out the other day, I may say I should always be glad to be her confederate in anything—one of the few times in my life, Edna, I was actually sorry to leave your house. No, I did not go to your safe, although I am interested to know that you have one."

"That's where they were," said Edna indignantly, looking round. "The pearls were locked up in the safe. I know that."

"Like so much of your more positive information, my dear, that, too, is wrong," said Conway. "You had them on when I called. And as we talked they came unfastened, and you took them off and laid them on the table beside you. Something told me that you had not been aware of what you did, and so when you refused so very roughly to lend me the sum of money I needed I simply took back my pearls—when you were not looking."

"Gordon," said Edna, "you stole my pearls." And her tone had a note of triumph as if the old delight of putting him in the wrong had not entirely died.

"I took my pearls from the table," said Conway, "and turned them for a few days into cash, with which I know you will be glad to know I made a lot of money—a pot of money, Albertson—there is money still to be made on the races for a smart fellow who knows how; and then, my dear, with a quixotic impulse I gave you the pearls, as I have always thought of doing. Some men might have given them to a younger and more amiable woman, but my nature has always been distinguished by a peculiar form of loyalty. I give them to you—for the sake of old times."

"You brought them back for the sake of not going to jail," said Edna, her eyes flashing at him. He smiled gently.

"Edna," he said, "as time goes on you learn nothing—absolutely nothing. Durland, when are you going to begin to grow? Good night, Albertson. Remember that you are a witness to this gift. Good night."

And he had taken his departure before anyone spoke again. It was Durland who spoke first. His voice shook a little.

"You see, mother," he said, "what a terrible injustice you have done Miss Exeter. She might sue you, only she's too generous. Oh, if you had only told me that my father had been about that day—only you never tell me anything, as if I were a baby. You will apologize to her, won't you?"

"I do not seem to be likely to get the chance of speaking to her at all," said Edna, glancing at the closed door.

Cora Wellington rose to her feet.

"I'm sorry to be inhospitable, Edna," she said, "but I have had a long, hard day attending to your business, and I want to go to bed. In fact, I think I'll go." And she walked firmly out of the room and upstairs, where, since the house—like the Conways'—was lightly built, she could be heard rapidly walking about on her heels in the room immediately overhead.

"Well," said Mr. Albertson, "It looks like I may as well be getting back to the Great White Way myself. I congratulate you on the happy termination of this affair, Mrs. Conway. I do not think that emerald is genuine, but I presume it is the sentiment that will appeal to you. I feel as happy as you do that that sweet young lady is as innocent as a baby."

It cannot be said that Edna looked particularly happy over this point. She raised her shoulders.

"But we don't know yet who she is. She certainly is not Miss Exeter."

Albertson smiled.

"You will find it was just a girlish prank," he said. "And I think we may presume that Mr. Wood now knows the whole story. I think if you'll permit me I'll call my assistant and we will get the car and be off."

Mrs. Conway, once again wearing her pearls, and Durland, still talking of apologies, accompanied Mr. Albertson back to the other house.

So the room was empty. Gradually it seemed to lose even the remembrance of its late occupants. The down cushion of the chair in which Edna had been sitting rose softly to its accustomed level with something like a sigh of relief. A wicker sofa, of stiffer nature, creaked in every fibre. A drooping flower in a glass vase gave a little shiver and shed every last petal on the table, as if it had been waiting all the evening to do this. Even the window curtains ceased swaying in the sea-breeze. It was as if the room and everything in it settled down to a breathless expectancy.

And at last the door of the little room opened and Pearl and Anthony came out. They did not appear at all surprised to find the room empty. They would not have been surprised to find the universe empty—to hear phantom newsboys calling an extra announcing that no one existed but themselves—"Rumor confirmed that only Pearl and Anthony Exist."

Pearl looked about her with that beautiful starry blankness that certain emotions bring to any human countenance—a thousand times starrier than ever before.

"I wonder," she said, without the slightest trace of real interest, "what has happened."

"Haven't you been listening to me," said Anthony. "A miracle has happened—we have fallen in love."

Nevertheless he understood her meaning; and just to please her he walked to the door and glanced into the corridor. It was as essentially empty as the room. Then as he returned to her, although she was staring in the opposite direction and he made not the slightest sound on the thick rug, she turned her face slowly up and over her shoulder, and met his lips with hers. Nor did either of them mention this as a miracle or even an example of uncharted psychic powers.

It was a long kiss; an inexperienced onlooker might have thought it a quiet ritual rather than a manifestation of human passion. When it was over, they stood once more in complete silence. Then Pearl said:

"I think we ought to go back to our sister's house."

"I suppose so," said Anthony. And again by an apparently mystical understanding they moved not across the lawn toward Mrs. Conway's house, but out across the dunes toward the beach.

There was no moon, but the milky way like a narrow cloud rose straight out of the sea, and the Scorpion was brightly festooned above the southern horizon.

Milton Keynes UK
Ingram Content Group UK Ltd.
UKHW050650260624
444769UK00004B/197